SHORT STACK

By Sharon A. Cantor

All rights reserved. No part of this book may be reproduced, scanned, or distributed in any printed or electronic form without permission. Please purchase only authorized editions.

While suggested by true events, this is a work of fiction. Names, characters, places, and incidents either are the product of the author's imagination or are used fictitiously, and any resemblance to persons, living or dead, businesses, companies, events, or locales, is entirely coincidental.

Text Copyright © 2015
Sharon A. Cantor
All rights reserved

ISBN:9781508887799

Life in the Eastern Tennessee mountains in the 1800's is as dangerous and unpredictable as it is beautiful and untamed. Young Kelly Ann McDaniels, known to everyone as 'Short Stack', has to grow up quickly as she finds herself locked in a battle for survival between the harsh elements of each passing winter, an ongoing and bitter war over land between the U. S. government and Native Americans, and the callous greed of ruthless intruders threatening her mountain home. Will Short Stack's fiery grit and determination be enough to help keep her and her family alive and safe?

"...a compelling page-turner ... thrilling and heartfelt ... filled with unforgettable characters that come alive on the page, Ms. Cantor successfully captures a time and place rich with natural beauty and fraught with danger ... "
~ Walt Hicks, publisher/editor of HellBound Books Publishing

Sharon A. Cantor is also the author of *Two Hearts, One Song*, available at Amazon.com.

Dedications

First and foremost, I dedicate this book to my identical twin brothers:
Ray Earl White & Ralph Benton White

I also dedicate this book to my grandsons Elliott M. Waterbury and Devon L. Waterbury.

Contents

Acknowledgements   xi

CHAPTER 1 *The Land of Milk and Honey*   *13*
CHAPTER 2 *The Patience of Job*   *23*
CHAPTER 3 *The Wilcox Family*   *33*
CHAPTER 4 *Austenaco Cherokee "Chief"*   *47*
CHAPTER 5 *New Arrivals on the Mountain*   *61*
CHAPTER 6 *Grace of Truth*   *73*
CHAPTER 7 *Day of Judgment*   *83*
CHAPTER 8 *Evil Spirits*   *93*
CHAPTER 9 *The Mountain Man*   *103*
CHAPTER 10 *Trouble on the Mountain*   *113*
CHAPTER 11 *Dancing Butterflies*   *127*
CHAPTER 12 *A Big Ole Rattler*   *139*
CHAPTER 13 *Betrayed*   *151*
CHAPTER 14 *The Loss of Adahy*   *163*
CHAPTER 15 *Trail of Tears*   *173*
CHAPTER 16 *Ross' Landing*   *183*
CHAPTER 17 *Abandoned Cabins*   *195*
CHAPTER 18 *Meet Your Maker*   *205*
CHAPTER 19 *Answered Prayer*   *217*
CHAPTER 20 *Coming Home*   *229*
CHAPTER 21 *No More Secrets*   *243*
CHAPTER 22 *Cherokee Roses*   *255*

About the Author   **271**

Acknowledgements

My heartfelt appreciation to Walt Hicks for his many hours of editing, formatting and encouragement.

*Cover & cover page illustration:
Artist Suzi Lockwood Hanscom*

CHAPTER 1
The Land of Milk and Honey

I was born in the middle of spring, 1814, right around the time Ole General Andrew Jackson was wearin' down the Creek Indians during the Battle of Horseshoe Bend down in Tehopeka, Alabama. I come from up yonder, just below the ridge of those mountains up there, just a stone's throw from the Appalachian Trail snakin' through Eastern Tennessee. This is my land—I know it like the back of my hand, every inch of it. Ain't nothin' happens in these parts that I don't get wind of it. This mountain and me belong together just like two peas in a pod.

My Pa, Jethro McDaniels hailed from British soil, but he made it known to folks he never gave a lick for royalty, they were just too damn uppity. Wealth and land would go to a body's head faster than a jack rabbit with a hound dog hot on its heels. The common folks back in the old country had no choice—they toiled 'neath the burden of heavy taxation and prayed for deliverance. The meager wages of the poor could not balance the scales of power and justice under the British crown.

Pa felt the itch and listened to the whispers of a New World, a virtual Garden of Eden. There was a vast wilderness to be conquered in the New World with the promise of land and freedom, if you had the gumption for the adventure. On many a starry night around the campfire, passing the bottle amongst the menfolk, there was considerable fat to chew on. There was a chance to escape, if only for a little while, with all that talk of the New World. Amidst the old men already settled with their families, there were also the wild, adventurous young men eagerly chomping at the bit for the challenge of the unknown New World. It gave some menfolk hope—it gave some a way out—and others a small glimpse of a dream they would have to live without.

Instead of standing on the shoreline and imagining what lay beyond the horizon of the waves, Pa would end up traveling across a vast blue ocean to tame an unbroken land of milk and honey. Pa was young enough to take a chance for a better life in the New World.

SHORT STACK

My Pa wanted a life with his own land so he could plant his own crops, harvest his own fields and keep his own wealth, but the love of a young girl held his fancy. He could not bring himself to leave without the young woman who had stolen his heart. Jethro wanted a big family with a passel of young'uns, and his heart was set on Beverly Ann.

On a warm spring day, with the first tiny buds of leaves growing on the trees, Jethro McDaniels proposed to Beverly Ann Davis. Gallantly, he gently took her hand, and as he gazed into her hazel eyes, he nervously stuttered, "I...I don't have much, but I do expect to prosper. If you would be so obliged."

Jethro swallowed hard as he immediately dropped to one knee, continuing his proposal. "Beverly Ann, I am up and asking for your hand in holy matrimony. I got to be honest, I ain't got no wedding ring nor do I have the pounds to buy one."

Jethro quickly rose from his knee and took her into his massive arms. "I do have this here gold locket. It belonged to my Ma. I know she would be right proud if you were wearing it."

Beverly was beautiful, the perfect portrait of a young girl in love, her long, light brown hair glistening in the sun as it fell upon her shoulders.

She had big hazel eyes, long black eyelashes shyly giving off a flirtatious flutter when she batted her eyes.

Her heart was pounding. She couldn't quite catch her breath as she looked into the deep blue eyes of Jethro McDaniels. He was so handsome, long black hair and a muscular six foot four inch frame with massive shoulders. His blue eyes danced with laughter and love. Beverly Ann would soon be a new bride and accompany her husband to the New World: the Land of Milk and Honey.

Jethro worked hard and saved each pound he made until he had secured passage for his bride. He had arranged with the captain of the vessel to work as a boat hand during the voyage in order to secure his own passage. Jethro had little time to spend with Beverly once the ship pulled up anchor, and the wind filled the sails. It was hard work aboard ship, and everyone had to pull their own weight. Weeks into the passage, the trip became increasingly unbearable—morale was downright lower than a snake's belly in a wagon rut.

There was hunger, scurvy, and thirst. Then came an unknown fever aboard ship, which the crew blamed on rats that had crept aboard at the dock. Jethro McDaniels and his new bride would reach the New World, but they would feel the hardship of each person as if it were their own trial by fire.

Watching children being buried at sea was the most horrific. It was god-awful to watch a child suffer from the fever for weeks, and bearing witness to a child unable to hold broth down left a body feeling helpless. It was a downright shame to watch a child no bigger than a corn nubbin wilt away to near nothing. In the end, their kinfolk could do nothing but bid a sorrowful goodbye as their beloved child was embraced forever by the sea.

I was downright lucky to grow up in East Tennessee with two brothers and two sisters beneath the Blue Ridge Mountains, along the Nolichucky River, a couple of country miles from the Appalachian Trail. In the original Cherokee language, the name of the river Nolichucky roughly translates to "spruce tree place." The Cherokee believed the river was possessed with evil spirits. Some said the river was the devil's looking glass, but Pa told me the river just had a life of its own, with strong currents and a bad undertow. I never ventured far from shore when I would sneak down to the river to cool off on a hot summer day. I enjoyed the cool water when I could just play and explore the shoreline, but taking a bath in the river made me a mite uneasy—Ma always made me take off *all* my clothes.

There were no neighbors within shouting or walking distance. The closest settlement was a good four day journey by foot—two days by horseback—so a body took care not to offend their kinfolk since there was no one else for miles around to talk to. A family had to stick together like fleas on a hound dog's back.

Together we shared the burden of work in order to survive on the mountain. But once the chores were all done, and the sun would start melting into the Tennessee sky just beyond the Blue Ridge Mountains, Pa would tell us stories about the mountain. Sometimes, he would just take a notion to play his fiddle. The sweet sound of that old fiddle harmonized with the distant echo of our voices resounding against the valley walls of the mountain as we sang and danced in the twilight. The crickets began to sing their song with the approaching fall of darkness, and the fireflies came to life to light up the night sky.

The night shadows danced on the ground, clinging to the slow burning coals of our campfire. When the voices of children floated through the air on the lilt of laughter, a body could feel the love and unity of family. The moon rising in the sky above us would betray our laughter and songs with each passing hour. It was always difficult to convince five wide-eyed children it was time for bed, but when Pa laid down his fiddle without a word spoken, five reluctant children put on their night shirts and went to bed.

Our way of life on the mountain was simple, untouched by the outside world with its cruelties of human nature. We didn't have much as far as worldly possessions, but I don't recall ever feeling poor. We lived in a thickset log cabin Pa built with his own two hands. There was plenty of water and a steady supply of food, and Ma did a right fine job of making our clothes.

When spring arrived on the mountain, the warm breath of life created colorful blossoms on the fruit trees. The mountain was saturated in sunshine and the astounding colors of wildflowers that would take your breath away.

Pa would plow the rich Tennessee earth so Ma could plant her vegetable garden. I never took to mind why Ma called it 'her' garden, because we all worked it. Pulling them weeds that grew faster than the vegetables was not one of my favorite chores. However, tending to Ma's garden did have a few agreeable rewards.

By midsummer, I would be sneaking into the garden to pull sweet red tomatoes from the vine.

Once in awhile, Ma would yell at me for sneaking into the garden, but always leavened with a sense of humor. "Short Stack, I know you must want to pull weeds something fierce, else you wouldn't be sneaking into the garden at this time of day. Thank you for being so helpful. Now, take a good look yonder at the corn row down on the end."

Ma had a green thumb. She could make anything grow and before the first frost of autumn, she would have dried and stored enough vegetables to last us all winter.

Pa cared for the few farm animals we raised for our meat, but each of us took our turn with chores when it came to feeding and fetching fresh water from the river for the animals. With the onset of winter, the livestock we tended would provide our meat through the cold months of snow and ice, when the mountain was the most unforgiving. Our survival depended on so many things—fishing the river, hunting the woods, trapping beaver and Ma's vegetable garden.

Pa loved the serenity of the woods, and the colorful displays of nature complemented the sights and sounds of God's creatures. After a good day of hunting, Pa would always come walking up to the cabin with a quick step to his feet. A broad grin would spread across his face as he held his trophy high into the air.

SHORT STACK

I spent endless childhood hours with him, walking in the woods beyond the ridge. I loved to watch and listen to the animals that lived there: the constant chatter of a squirrel, the high-pitched cry of a bobwhite quail, the piercing scream of an eagle, and the soft whimper of a newborn fawn.

Pa taught me to respect the beauty of the mountain and its dangers. By the time I was half again as high as a beanpole, I could mimic most of the animals on the mountain. I loved the sound of the wind whispering through the trees. I loved to breathe deeply of the delicate fragrance carried by the wind before a summer rainstorm, when the trees would turn their leaves over in defiance of the approaching rain. The mountain was my home.

Ma just didn't understand the woods or the animals that lived there. She didn't think it was very ladylike to go traipsing around in the woods. "It just isn't safe," Ma would say. "A body could get hurt. Or ruin a perfectly good dress." But, I didn't much cotton to dresses or being ladylike. And early on, I wasn't much scared of getting hurt. I was downright contented in them woods.

I was taught wisely from the time I was born to respect the Good Book. It was the only book Ma really ever cottoned to. We had other reading books from time to time, but I wasn't much for book learning. In the woods beyond the ridge, I could see and feel what Ma only read about in those pages from her Bible, the very Presence of God. I remember a story in the Bible Ma read to us about a man named Job, who lost everything he owned, everyone he loved and even endured a terrible sickness, but still Job did not turn away from his God.

    I wasn't near as strong as Job when the evil men came down the mountain.

CHAPTER 2
The Patience of Job

I reckon that day will always be lurking somewhere in the back of my mind, hiding just out of sight, until something or someone at last recalls that page of my life right out of the past. I have never considered myself to be a strong sort, but time and circumstances proved me to be, if not strong, at least enduring. I guess a body will never understand or grasp what they have the sand to do, until they are forced to stand on their own two feet and do it. A trial by fire creates panic, fear and doubt, but you find yourself walking through the fire and doing it with a right smart amount of gumption when your own survival—or that of your family—demands it from you.

At first, I thought an eagle was screaming somewhere high above me, but searching the clear blue sky, my heart skipped a beat as another scream pierced the silence of my soul. I made fast tracks for the cabin, but then I stopped and hid at the edge of the woods just out of sight, with Pa's wisdom ringing in my ears:

"Girl, don't be walking into trouble without knowing what you're up against. That wouldn't make no sense at all."

I could hear Ma and my sisters screaming. When the front door of the cabin door flew open, my eyes focused on the strange man who suddenly appeared there. My heart near burst with a sudden surge of terror and injustice. From what I could see, they were four trappers: a bad sort, from the other side of the mountain. I watched helplessly as they dragged my father from the cabin. It took three of 'em to hold Pa down while another savagely beat him, landing one blow after another until his face was battered and bloody. At that moment, I prayed for lightning bolts to strike those bad men down, but God refused to listen. I stared in disbelief as one of the trappers raised his rifle and aimed that long black barrel at Pa. The discharge of that bullet roared like the trapped scream of disbelief within my heart as the shot echoed through the hills and valleys surrounding the mountain.

From where I was sitting, I could see as clear as spring water, there wasn't nary a thing I could do. Pa was lying face down in front of the cabin. I knew Pa was in a bad way—maybe dead, and Ma was trying to put up a fight against four trappers. She fought like a mountain wildcat, but Ma was no match for them. As those men dragged Ma into the cabin, I watched, feeling helpless, for I didn't lift a finger to help her. I will live with that guilt until the day I die.

I couldn't see my sisters from where I was hunkered down, so I slipped up to the back of the cabin. From there, I could hear the tortured cries of my sisters, begging the trappers to stop hurting Ma. Angry tears ran down my face as I listened to the frightened voices of my sisters. Again, I prayed for lightning bolts, but God still did not answer my prayers. I covered my ears with my hands to block out the constant sound of my brothers and sisters screaming and crying.

A river of tears flowed down my face, but no sound escaped my lips as my whole body trembled from fear. The shadows of night were beginning to fall across the cabin when I noticed Pa's rifle. He had fallen on top of it during the fight. I went silent as the night, sneaking up to Pa. He moaned softly when I pulled the rifle from underneath him. Pa was still alive. I tried with grim determination to pull him into the cover of the woods, but he was just too big for me to pull very far. I will always remember what Pa said to me that night.

"Short Stack, you're going on fourteen years. You know the mountain girl, and you got the smarts and grit to help your Ma. But you only got one shot in that rifle, so don't you go and do anything foolhardy."

Pa tried to tell me more, but he just drifted away in my arms. His eyes were open, staring into nothing except the gathering dusk of evening when he died. Intently, I studied my father as I cradled him gently in my arms, not wanting to forget a single line of his face, not wanting to close his eyes. I relinquished after a few minutes, finally gently closing his eyes with my hand, angry tears flowing down my face. I did not want to say goodbye or face the cruel reality I would never again see those eyes of wisdom shining down at me with love. At that moment, I couldn't remember ever feeling so scared or helpless. But I also wanted retribution—pure hatred was burning a hole through my heart.

From inside the cabin, I could hear the sounds of scuffling now and again. The night wind was cool, but I could feel the drops of sweat trickling down my backside. I listened to my twin brothers as they cried, and it gave me a thread of hope. They were only going on their third year. I ached to go in shooting Pa's gun, but I knew I might just get the rest of them killed. I had to wait outside the cabin, hoping the trappers wouldn't kill again.

The sun was just kissing the mountain ridge good night, when the cabin door slammed wide open. Standing in the doorway was a man as big as an old black bear, but even a scruffy old bear fresh from a bramble bush would have been a damn sight prettier. He stretched and yawned, scratching his back on the inside of the cabin door.

I had never known such hate. I carefully aimed the rifle with the big man dead in my sights. At that moment, I could have killed him, but I heard the frightened voices of my brothers. They were still alive, so I had no choice but to lower my rifle instead of putting a bullet between that blackguard's beady eyes.

All four men were now standing out in the open. I squeezed Pa's gun so tight my hands turned white. I watched them walk back into our cabin one last time. The trappers stole whatever they could find: a silver teapot, Ma's gold locket and Pa's beaver pelts.

I watched as they mounted their horses. The big ugly one laughed and dangled Ma's gold locket. Pa had given it to her back in their courting days. I wanted to shoot him right out of the saddle, but I was forced to stay in the cover of the woods with enough hate burning inside me to explode the mountain.

I listened to the pounding hooves of their horses, waiting for the sound to fade. When I could no longer hear the clatter of hoofbeats, I crawled to the nearest tree, and braced myself against the side of it, slowly struggling to my feet. My legs felt weak from sitting, trembling beneath the weight of my own body. The only sound coming from the cabin was the tormented cries of my brothers.

It seemed like I was walking slow as an old box turtle, but I was moving just as fast as I could muster. Slow as molasses, I opened the cabin door with a trembling hand and my stomach turning inside out. My brothers bolted across the room with their little hands reaching for me in desperation, but then I took in enough air to nearly choke the very life from me, gagging on every breath, when I saw the faces of my sisters, Elizabeth and Kimberly. They were lying just inside the cabin door.

Elizabeth was the eldest, she was seventeen. She was as cute as a newborn fawn and smart with book learning, too. Ma thought she should have spent more of her time looking for a husband instead of keeping her nose in a book. Elizabeth had set her mind to teach book learning to children. I can't say as I blame her none: most of the men who ever came courting were from the trading post or the settlement, and there wasn't a one of them that I would have cottoned to. Kimberly Ann was sixteen and just as smart as Elizabeth when it came to book learning, but Kimberly Ann was on the plump side and, truth to be told, just a shade on the homely side, too. Kimberly wanted to find a husband and raise a family on the mountain to be near her kinfolk. Neither one of them would ever see the sun crest the ridge of the mountain again.

I stumbled through the cabin door, dragging both of my brothers who refused to let go of me. Blinded by my own tears, I reached for the closest tree to keep myself from falling, taking in several deep, ragged breaths. Then I got sick. There was nothing inside me, but my guts churned and retched all the same. When the sickness passed and I regained a little control, I walked back inside the cabin.

I untied the hands of my sisters and pulled the cloths from their mouths. I covered their naked bodies and then looked for Ma. I found her lying beside her bed. Maybe I should have looked for Ma before I tended to my sisters, but something inside of me knew Ma was already dead, and I just did not want to face the truth.

When I touched her, Ma felt so cold. I gently picked her up in my arms and hugged her. She was a true lady, and she didn't need a fancy gown of silk to prove it. I held her in a dreamlike state of mind until the screams of my brothers brought me back to reality. I dragged Ma and my sisters outside and laid them down next to Pa. I pulled blankets from their beds and covered their bodies from the hot sun. All four of them had been scalped by white men who would use those scalps to collect a bounty of blood money.

I reckon the trappers left my brothers alive believing they would just die being left all alone, or if'n someone did happen to stumble onto them, the boys were just too young to talk. I had to dig four graves that day, but first my brothers needed to be taken care of. I can tell you, it was a mighty eerie feeling fixing supper for my brothers with most of my family lying dead in front of the cabin.

It took me the better part of the following morning to quiet down the twins and get them to sleep before I could dig the graves. The twins had seen everything. I can only imagine the nightmare they had witnessed. I was afraid the vultures would start to circle before I could get my folks buried proper. Those birds are evil. I would not suffer the torment of even the cold flesh of my loved ones being torn into by the talons of hell. I buried them right alongside of the cabin. I couldn't pull Pa any farther. It was almost nightfall before I hammered the last wooden cross in place.

I went back inside the cabin and got Ma's Bible. It was all I could think of to do. Carefully, I began to read just the way Ma had taught me.

"The Lord is my Shepherd. I shall not want. He leadeth me into the path of righteousness for His namesake. He leadeth me beside the still waters."

It was then I felt the blood on my hands. Ma's Bible was covered with it.

"I promise Pa, though I walk through the valley of the shadow of death, I will fear no evil, until I see them ugly bastards dangling from a rope—a mountain rope, Pa!"

By the time I had calmed down and the tears had subsided, the twins were awake again. My whole body ached for sleep, but I knew I couldn't. I fed my brothers. I fetched in water from the creek, bathed them and put clean nightshirts on them. I played games with my brothers as though nothing had happened. When the twins had finally closed their eyes to sleep, I felt my body begin to tremble.

Fresh tears spilled over my quivering body.

The hate inside me felt like the hot smoldering coals of a forest fire that had finally ignited into a raging inferno. The flames of hate and grief consumed my heart, burning away the loneliness and fear. I cried until another tear refused to fall. Exhaustion slowly crept into my body as I faded off to sleep, praying for the courage, the wisdom and the patience of Job.

CHAPTER 3
The Wilcox Family

The next morning, the twins were awake at the crack of dawn. They decided to playfully rouse me from my restless night of dreams by jumping up and down on my bed, giggling with mischief until I screamed, "Clayton! Catlin! Get off this here bed right now, before I bust your backsides!" Their laughter faded into silence after I yelled at them. The look of fear in their eyes made me feel downright pitiful and ashamed. I got up and hugged them both.

I tried patiently to fix breakfast with the young'uns hanging onto me, crying to be fed. I was getting more than a little flustered with them both, but seeing the look on their little faces when they tasted my pancakes made the endurance worth it. Ma had always done the cooking and to tell the truth, I just wasn't much good at it. My first attempt at pancakes turned out too lumpy, a little too much flour in the batter, I figured. Some of them were slightly burned—a little too much wood burning in the fireplace.

After I fed my brothers, they settled down on the floor to play with some little wooden toys Pa had carved for them. I opened the cabin door and took a look around outside. I felt the warmth of the sun upon my face and gazed at a clear blue Tennessee sky. The sweet scent of wild mountain flowers carried on the wind that gently tousled my hair. I breathed deeply of the mountain air and then looked back at my brothers. I realized there would be times when I would want to cuss—Pa did that sometimes. There would be moments when I would become downright discouraged and cry. There would be times when I would just want to throw my hands in the air and give up. The way I looked at it, I could cry a river if I really needed too, but I could never give up. I needed to protect my brothers and our mountain home.

One of the first chores at hand was to check Pa's ammunition supply. I wanted the opportunity to fire more than one shot from the rifle if'n I needed to. I would have to practice some on the reloading, as the timing of a reload could be critical in any situation. Pa kept his ammunition stored under a loose board in the cabin floor located about two feet from the right side of the fireplace. The trappers hadn't found it. If they ever took a notion to come back, I would make them regret their actions. In Pa's secret hiding place, I discovered enough black powder and musket balls to hold off a small army, if'n I used it wisely. I also found nine gold pieces that Pa had been saving for supplies. I would have to be careful with the money and the ammunition.

The thought did cross my mind to attempt a journey with the boys and take them down the mountain, but where would we go? We had no kin that I could recall except for Pa's brother David, and the last I heard tell of him, he was somewhere down around North Carolina. I had no way of tracking him down, and I can't say I really wanted to, since the mountain was my home. I would just have to set my mind to prepare for the coming winter just like my folks had always done. We didn't stand a chance of making it through the bitter cold winter ahead of us, if I didn't.

The list of chores I needed to do was endless, with livestock and two little brothers to care for. I needed to fetch mud from the creek and patch the cracks in between the logs of the cabin, I needed to dry and store vegetables, and I needed to chop enough wood to make it through the winter. There was just too much work for one pair of hands to do. Pa had already prepared our meat. It was quartered and hanging in the smokehouse curing.

Some folks might have thought it was a mite unkind, but I couldn't keep a good watch over the twins while I was working in the garden or chopping wood. So I built a small fenced-in area—I reckon you could call it a pen—for my brothers to play in while I worked. After a spell, the twins seemed to get used to the idea and stayed put without a fuss. I have to admit, it was hard at first, listening to them cry for me. More times than I could shake a stick at, when they cried for me, I had to turn away so they wouldn't see me cryin', too. My brothers were just too young to understand all the painful memories that haunted me. All they wanted was to be held and loved, but I only had two hands. The work that needed to be done for our survival demanded my immediate and nearly constant attention.

Not many folks came by the cabin, except maybe soldiers or folks that knew Pa from the settlement or settlers passing along the Appalachian Trail to the other side of the mountain. The supplies that were left would have to see us through the winter. I would have to store as many vegetables as I could before winter, and then make do with what we had. It would be spring before anyone might come calling. Maybe by then, Ole Man Warner from the trading post might start wondering why Pa hadn't come down the mountain to trade his pelts.

Pa had trapped the river for pelts, mostly beaver, since I was no bigger than a corn nubbin. The money from the pelts provided the supplies we needed like coffee, sugar and flour. Pa would make the two-day journey on horseback to the trading post before the first snow to fetch back the supplies we needed. It took a mite longer to get to the trading post with the horses pulling the wagon. I knew taking that trip would be impossible with the twins, and even if I could have managed the trip, there were no pelts to trade for the supplies we needed.

Considering everything the three of us had been through, the twins seemed to be faring well, and I still felt determined. My brothers did not seem to notice that the rest of the family was gone, and every now and again, Catlin and Clayton would call me Ma. The first time I heard one of them say it, I have to admit, I felt real funny about it, but I figured it was a compliment of sorts—Ma was a real fine woman. When my brothers were old enough to understand, I'd have them call me Short Stack, just like Ma had done.

Several months passed by before I saw anyone. I was tired, frustrated and lonely. One day while I was chopping wood in front of the cabin, I heard the creak of wagon wheels and the crackling sound of the autumn leaves being crushed underneath the weight of the heavy-loaded covered wagon. I grabbed Pa's gun straight away—after what I had been through, I wasn't about to take no chance with strangers. I let them see Pa's rifle peeking at them through the crack of the front door of the cabin. After I could see with my own eyes they were ordinary folks, I lowered my gun. The first visitors to sit at our table and stay on a spell turned out to be the Wilcox family, settlers headed for the Mississippi Valley.

I stepped through the cabin door with Pa's gun still in my right hand, but with a relaxed grip on the stock of the rifle. The man driving the heavy-loaded wagon smiled at me. Nigh as I could tell from a distance, there was a man and a woman sitting on the front seat of the wagon. He appeared to be slender, probably around six-foot, give or take an inch. His hair was a sun-lit brown that accented his dark brown eyes. Once they got closer, I heard a profound spirit of goodness in his voice.

"Howdy, there. My name is Jason Wilcox. This here is my wife Velma and my son Johnny."

It was nice to hear another voice coming back at me instead of just listening to my own voice talking to Clayton and Catlin.

SHORT STACK

Velma smiled timidly as she asked, "Are your folks about?"

I tried to force a smile and slowly shook my head. "My folks died a while back, but this here is my brothers Catlin and Clayton. My name is Short Stack."

I fumbled for something else to say, feeling awkward as her crystal blue eyes searched mine. "I got some rabbit stew cookin' on the fireplace, if you're a mind to stay for supper—there's plenty, huntin' was good this morning."

Velma wasn't much good at hiding her feelings, come to think of it, neither was Ma. I saw the concerned look in her eyes as she started to climb down from the wagon.

"That's right nice of you, Short Stack—we'd be obliged. I can lend a hand and rustle up some biscuits to go with the stew."

They were right sorry about my kin and offered to stay on a spell to help me out before they traveled on. Johnny chopped wood and helped me fetch mud and small stones from the river bed to patch the cabin for winter. He was sixteen, but looked much older than his years. He was muscular and tall, standing an easy six foot in his socking feet, but he was fair like his ma, with hair the color of the golden daffodils that grew wild in the valley below the mountain.

Velma fell in love with the twins and spoiled them something awful. I hate to admit it, but sometimes I got a little jealous of her because she knew exactly how to handle the twins. It was difficult for me, as I was their sister, but trying to be like Ma.

The Wilcox family had been with me going on three weeks, and I could feel Jason was growing restless—he wanted to move on. I can't say I blame him none. They had come a far piece and they still had a long journey ahead of them. The cabin was ready for winter, and we had apples, peaches, wild berries and vegetables dried and stored up for the winter. I was aching to spend some time in the woods before they moved on, so after supper that night, I found the courage to up and ask Johnny if he would like to go hunting in the morning. Johnny looked at me with a dumb grin on his face, laughter dancing in his eyes.

"Short Stack, did your Pa ever take you hunting?"

I didn't cotton to that dumb grin on his face and to tell the truth, I was of a sudden mad as a little wet hen, but Johnny and his family had done right by me and my brothers.

"Pa took me hunting lots of times. I know these woods like the back of my hand. I'll be up before first light if you have a mind to go with me."

Johnny and I were in the woods at the crack of dawn. Velma watched over the boys for me while I was gone. It was the first time I had been in the woods for any length of time since the death of my family. I felt the crisp autumn wind blow against my face and listened to the wildlife awaken around me, and then I thought about Pa. The long walks I had taken with him seemed like a lifetime ago.

I carried Pa's gun with pride. Pa had taught me to shoot and sit a horse just as good as any man. Velma didn't think it was proper for a lady to go off hunting in the woods. It just wasn't ladylike, she said. She sounded a lot like Ma. I have to be honest, her words cut deep and she was becoming a thorn in my side. I didn't really cotton to her lecturing me about being more of a lady. Ma had said the same, but Velma wasn't Ma. I had to keep telling myself: *they've done right by you and your brothers—keep your mouth shut.*

"Kelly Ann is such a lovely name. Why did your family call you Short Stack?" Velma hadn't meant to hurt my feelings, but without a doubt, she had sure enough ruffled my feathers.

"I'm right proud of my name. Pa gave it to me—said I was short, but I was stacked right up to size."

Maybe it was the tone of my voice, or maybe it was the flash of anger that clearly showed in my eyes, but Velma knew she had tread on my feelings. Timidly, she smiled. "I'm sorry, Short Stack. You should be right proud of the name your Pa gave you, but your long auburn hair is so pretty. I could show you how to curl it, if you take a mind to. You would be a fine looking young lady in a dress with your hair curled."

I knew Velma was a fine, well-meaning woman, so I kept my thoughts to myself. I didn't have time to be a lady—I had to take care of my brothers and our home, and I sure as hell couldn't do that in a dress.

Johnny and I were walking quiet-like through the woods, long before the sun crested the mountain ridge. The sun couldn't've been up for more than an hour as we continued south of the cabin, when suddenly I saw Johnny stop straightaway in front of me. Slowly, he lifted his rifle, braced it against his shoulder and took aim. My eyes searched the woods. It didn't feel right when I could see exactly what Johnny was aiming at.

It wasn't a good shot, so I placed my hand on his shoulder and whispered, "Johnny-boy, you better be a damn good shot to take that black bear from here. There ain't nothing meaner than a wounded bear."

Maybe Johnny took the shot because he thought I was just a squirt of a girl who didn't know what she was talking about. Maybe he fired his rifle because he truly believed he was a damn good shot. Either way, it didn't matter—now we had a downright mean, cantankerous, wounded bear on our hands. Johnny yelled for me to run, but I knew that even a wounded bear could outrun us both. My whole body trembled with fear, but I took a deep breath and stood my ground when the bear charged. I lifted my gun, braced it against my shoulder and took careful aim. I could hear Pa whispering in my ear with the wind, and I knew Pa was standing right next to me.

"Girl, that bear will get you for sure if you don't aim it straight! Don't bend your arm, Short Stack. Squeeze gentle-like on the trigger—don't jerk it, girl! Fire!"

It was over in a matter of seconds, but it seemed like it took forever. Johnny had this dumbfounded look on his face.

"Lord, girl, you ain't got no sense."

I half-heartedly smiled at him. "I got more than most, Pa said so."

Then I turned away, because I didn't want him to see the tears in my eyes or the uncontrolled nervous tremble running through my body.

Roughly, in a stern voice of courage I did not feel, I groused, "Grab the rope and your knife—it's bear-skinnin' time."

I could use the bearskin for a number of things, but I decided to make winter coats for my brothers. Ma had done all of the sewing and I truly dreaded this chore. I knew it was going to take me a lot longer than it would have taken Ma, but I set my mind to do it. Ma always looked so contented sitting in the rocking chair, softly humming a song, bringing the needle up and down, making each stitch with care. Velma gave me some thread and tried her best to show me how to sew before they moved on. I was all thumbs at first, but I kept at it until I patched together a coat for each of my brothers, and while the coats wasn't pretty, they would do well and good to keep the boys warm.

I felt mostly relieved, but at the same time a little troubled when the Wilcox family moved on. I knew once winter set in, I would see no one until spring. I really wanted to cry, but I didn't, I just set my mind to doing chores. I stood in front of the cabin with my brothers, and we watched them leave, waving until we couldn't see them anymore through the clouds of dust and leaves on the mountain trail. Taking in a deep breath, I went back to doing my chores.

SHORT STACK

Cooking supper that night, I was feeling a mite lonesome. I looked at the twins playing with a little wooden boat Pa had carved. I had to smile—both of them was the spittin' image of Pa. Catlin had taken the small wooden boat from Clayton's hands, and he didn't cotton to it. Clinton quickly grabbed it back and hit his brother up alongside the head with it.

They were growing like wildfire and that suited me right down to the ground. Someday they would be big enough to watch over me and take over this land. Catlin Ray McDaniels and Clayton Lee McDaniels would be men someday, mountain men.

CHAPTER 4
Austenaco Cherokee "Chief"

When the snow started falling on the mountain once again, I was prepared. I could relax a little and admire the snowfall's pale beauty. As I saw it, I had taken every possible precaution to protect my brothers. Soon, the mountain would be impossible to travel by wagon in the deep snow, and even on horseback, a body would have a rough time of it. The soft snowflakes would blanket the mountain in the glistening beauty of white danger. Ice storms would blow down the mountain, leaving behind layers of ice shining in the morning sun. Sheaths of ice would build until the heavily burdened branches broke beneath the weight. The bitter cold wind dancing atop the mountain's peak would slowly drift down the snow. The wind could drift the snow six to eight feet high during blizzards.

I didn't have to worry none about the trappers returning to the cabin with the onset of winter, or anyone else for that matter. My main concern was keeping my brothers safe and doing my best to keep the livestock warm, watered and fed. The snow drifts would make it difficult when it came to watering and feeding the livestock, but I would deal with crossing that bridge when I came to it.

I had no real idea of the passing of days, or even of the months to follow, as I watched the blinding white snow embrace the mountain. I was forced into learning to foretell the weather by watching the sky and judging the wind, just like Pa had done.

I wanted to celebrate Christmas with my brothers, but I really had no way of knowing exactly what day Christmas fell on. I finally decided to carve some wooden little toys for the twins from small pieces of red cedar I had come across in the woods. Once I finished the toys, we would celebrate Christmas.

Long, lazy hours passed by in front of the fireplace, carving on those little toys or playing games with my brothers. The twins were somewhat rowdy and irritable, as they didn't cotton to being cooped up in the cabin. Neither did I, but making the preparations for Christmas gave us all something to look forward to.

We celebrated Christmas Day about a month and a half after I had finished carving the wooden toys. I took down a nice size piece of venison from the smokehouse to cook for our holiday meal, and I made an apple pie from the dried apples I had put up before winter. I didn't have a lot of decorations for a Christmas tree, but that didn't really matter none—we would still have us a Christmas tree.

I bundled up Clayton and Catlin in warm clothes, their bearhide winter coats, and we set out to find a tree. I found a small pine tree not far from the cabin. The twins played in the snow, making snowballs to throw at each other, while I took on the task of cutting down the tree. The wind was kicking up some and it was cold, but the boys didn't seem to mind.

Even though the tree was small, and it was just a stone's throw from the cabin, it took me the better part of an hour to drag the tree back home. The twins were determined to help me drag the Christmas tree. It was side-splitting to watch the boys playing in the snow, falling and rolling down the hill. I could have gotten the tree into the cabin a lot quicker without them, but it was just more fun to let them help. After we reached the cabin and finally got the tree inside, I set the tree up against the far corner of the cabin, away from the fireplace.

My attention was then drawn back to my brothers. Clayton and Catlin were quickly becoming miserable in their cold, wet clothes, but shortly after the twins got warm and dry, they helped me place the few decorations we had onto the front of our Christmas tree. It made me feel a mite better to see the decorations Ma had collected and made through the years on our little Christmas tree.

That night after supper with the fire burning brightly in the fireplace, I popped some corn to string and told my brothers the story of baby Jesus. I would have read it to them from Ma's Bible, but I just couldn't understand some of the words. The twins were enjoying our celebration, but I had a hard time trying to make the twins understand I wanted the popcorn to decorate the Christmas tree—they just wanted to eat it.

Once my brothers were fast asleep, I sat by the soft glowing fire in Ma's rocker. I glanced above the fireplace and looked at Pa's fiddle hanging on the wall. Quietly I rose to my feet, reached for that old fiddle and pulled it down. Dust had settled on the slender body of the fiddle and the strings. Through misty eyes, I cleaned and polished Pa's old fiddle and placed it back over the fireplace.

The next morning the twins were awake just before daylight, all bright-eyed and bushy-tailed, ready to celebrate Christmas. The boys seemed to like their funny-looking wooden horses I had carved for them, and for the most part, I thought we had a nice Christmas. Our Christmas dinner of venison was a little tough, but the apple pie turned out just fine.

Catlin and Clayton were both starting to talk a lot more. Come spring they would turn four. Every afternoon after I put them down to sleep, I was out collecting Pa's traps. The traps needed to be cleaned, greased up and stored till spring. I had really meant to do this chore before the first snow, but I just ran out of daylight to complete this essential task.

The deep snow and ice covering the trails along the river slowed me down, but I finally managed to find most of the traps beneath the frozen coats of ice and snow. I cleaned the rust off the traps with moonshine and greased them up with bear fat. I was so glad I had tagged along with Pa while he was setting the traps and working them. Come spring, I would have to keep running the traps for beaver, for without the beaver pelts, I would have nothing to bargain with at the trading post.

I was getting more than a little anxious for spring to embrace the mountain. Impatiently, I waited for the snow to melt on the mountain, and I had a bad case of cabin fever that intensified with each passing day. Catlin and Clayton were just as fidgety and restless as I was, but they always seemed to keep each other occupied. Every morning, when I made my daily rounds of feeding and watering the animals, I would search the sky over the crest of the mountain ridge, wanting to see the season changing with a restless feeling in my heart. At times when it felt like the cabin walls were closing in on me, I wished I was more like Ma.

I don't know why I was in such a hurry for spring. There would be a garden to plant and tend, there would be traps to set and work along the river, and there wouldn't be enough hours in a day for me to complete the chores I needed to get done. When the warmth of spring finally arrived, I realized I could have waited awhile longer.

When the flowers started to bloom on the mountain, and the sweet scent of the laurel, honeysuckle and dogwood flowers poised their fragrances delicately in the air, I transplanted some of the flowers to the graves of my family.

SHORT STACK

Ma loved the wild mountain flowers, and somehow I felt a little closer to Ma when I kept the graves well-tended. Sometimes, I even talked to my folks as I tended to their graves. Whenever I got lonesome, it made me feel a mite better.

On one such afternoon, I was talking to Pa about running the traps along the river as I pulled weeds from his grave. Suddenly, I had the strangest feeling someone was watching me. I kept talking, but I reached for my rifle. My eyes searched the woods and then my heart skipped a beat. I could not believe my eyes.

I had heard stories about the Indian tribes in the territory from Pa, but I had never before laid eyes on an Indian up close and in the flesh. Cautiously, I began walking toward the trees with a tight grip on my rifle. I stopped about six yards from the edge of the trees, propped my arms across the top of my rifle and pushed back my hat. I just stood there not knowing what to do, when I heard the voice of wisdom.

"Short Stack, don't let him see the fear in your eyes. Stand up straight, girl and stare him down!"

When he stepped out of the trees and started walking toward me, my heart was beating a mite fast, but I stood my ground. Several moments went by in still silence. His long, shiny black hair held a small braid with brightly colored feathers woven into the braid. The dark eyes that searched mine showed neither fear nor concern. It seemed to be a stand-off, until I had an idea come to mind. I bowed politely toward him and stuck out my hand, hoping he would understand the gesture and take my hand. His eyes searched mine with curiosity and after several moments of curious hesitation, he took my hand. I smiled warmly at him and gently urged him with the motion of my hands to follow me.

Cautiously, I led him to the graves of my family. Beside my Pa's grave, I used both hands to draw lines of tears down my face and then pointed to the graves. I believe he understood what I was trying to show him, even though his eyes betrayed no emotion. Pa had taught me the graves of the dead were sacred ground to the Indian tribes. I had listened carefully to every story Pa ever told, and his words came easily to mind whenever I needed them most.

His attention was suddenly drawn toward the twins. Now, I was afraid. Sensing possible danger, my brothers began to cry. Slowly, he walked over to the fenced-in area I had built for Clayton and Catlin, moving toward the front of the cabin. When he first laid eyes on my brothers, the expression on his face was as still and unreadable as an old oak tree. To my surprise, he turned

SHORT STACK

toward me and smiled at me like an old friend, bowed politely and reached out his hand to me.

The fear was gone, and I smiled with the sun that was shining down on us, as my small hand disappeared into his strong handclasp. His curiosity seemed satisfied, and he started back towards the trees.

Of a sudden, he stopped and turned once more to face me. He placed his right hand across his chest and proudly shouted, "Austenaco!" I found out many moons later that his name meant "Chief" in the Cherokee language. He smiled and repeated "Austenaco!" Then he lifted his arm, pointed straight at me, and again placed his hand across his chest.

I positioned my hand across my chest just as he had done and cried loudly, "Short Stack!" He waved his hand in the air, nodded his head then disappeared into the woods like the early morning mist rolling down the mountain.

I did not see Austenaco again for almost two weeks. I had not even known he was there, but God Almighty, I'm sure glad he was. I surely would have been in a passel of trouble without him. I was down by the river checking traps. The river was high and swollen from the heavy snowfall that had melted and flowed fiercely down the mountain. Some of the traps were underwater just along the river's edge. I had to retrieve the traps and reset them on higher ground. I was searching for a trap when I slipped on the wet rocks. I fell headfirst onto a large boulder jutting from the river, which knocked both sense and wind right out of me. The river's current quickly took me before I could get my senses working again. I knew how to swim, but I was stunned, and the current was too fast and too powerful. I had already been swept a quarter of a mile downstream when my head finally began to clear. I gave it thunder, but no matter how hard I tried, I couldn't gain any ground against the vicious pull of the river. The river's current propelled me through the water as easily as a leaf caught in a windswept gale. I finally managed to grab hold of a large boulder and keep my head above water, long enough to rest a spell and try and figure out what I was going to do next. My options did not look good—I was stranded in the middle of the river with a powerful current keeping me from reaching shore on either side.

At the time, I thought my situation was hopeless. I felt like I had done gone and lost all my good sense. I was also scared to death—my brothers needed me, and I had allowed myself a moment of carelessness. I was giving myself a pretty rough time of it when I heard the sound of another voice, barely audible above the roar of the rushing water. I pulled myself up farther onto the rocks and peered over the top of the boulder. I saw Austenaco standing on the riverbank waving and yelling at me. I watched Austenaco rush over to his horse and retrieve a rolled up blanket. Inside the blanket was a coil of rope. He quickly fashioned the rope into a lasso. The first couple of times he tossed the rope through the air into the river, I couldn't reach it. Once, I almost lost my grip on the rocks trying to reach the rope. With a sudden chill I realized that if I ever managed to catch the rope, I would have no choice but to trust Austenaco to pull me to safety.

    I watched Austenaco spin the rope in the air once again, my eyes longingly following the path of the rope. Once it was within my reach, I didn't hesitate. My hands frantically clawed for the rope, and the rawhide rope felt rough, scrubbing the hide right off my hands, but I kept a good hold. With one hand, I held onto the boulder, as I used the other hand to pull the rope over my head and secure it just beneath my arms. I waited as Austenaco quickly tied off his end of the rope around his horse's broad neck. Austenaco signaled me from the shoreline he was ready, and I reluctantly let go of the rocks as he began to haul in the rope, easing his horse forward against my body weight and the fierce current.

By the time I reached shore, I was bruised and exhausted, but mighty thankful. The twins had been asleep when I left, but I had been gone a lot longer than I should have been. There was no telling what those boys might've gotten into with me gone.

Austenaco helped me back to the cabin, and I was thankful to be home and alive. But once I opened the cabin door, I wanted to beat the living daylights out of the twins. I know for a fact Pa would have wore them both out with a green switch.

From the look of the mess in the cabin, the twins had kept themselves occupied in my absence by having a pillow fight with Ma's feather pillows. Now they were sitting on the floor playing with the last jar of molasses we owned. I don't know how Catlin or Clayton ever managed to get it open, but one of them had, or they had done so together. Either way, there was molasses and feathers all over the twins and everywhere else I looked.

I stood there in the doorway of the cabin with Austenaco, feeling exhausted, wet, cold and hungry. I didn't know whether to laugh or to cry, so I laughed. Austenaco seemed highly amused, pointing at the twins and laughing gruffly. He made a gesture with his hands and arms, mimicking a very large bird in flight. My brothers found his bird dance quite hilarious and laughed with mischief as they imitated the movement of his arms.

I can't say I felt bad about giving my brothers a licking that day, as I had to clean up their mess, mend the pillows, fix supper and give them both a bath. The way I looked at it, they got off easy.

So had I.

CHAPTER 5
New Arrivals on the Mountain

With everything considered, I thought I was doing a good enough job of taking care of my brothers. Every now and again, I would find fresh meat and wild berries left outside our cabin door. Austenaco always helped us out after a good day of hunting. He believed the twins were blessed, something special. So did I, but then again, I was their sister.

Austenaco came by every once in awhile to check up on us and make sure we were faring well. One afternoon, while I was tending to the garden, he came by the cabin along with a young Indian girl, who couldn't have been much more than my age, give or take a year or two. She had long black hair and dark eyes and was as cute as a little speckled pup. She struck me as being on the timid side, so I didn't pay her much mind while I was conversing with Austenaco. Sometimes the hand signals we used in the place of talking couldn't convey the true and full meaning of what needed to be expressed. I had not understood Austenaco's intention to leave the young Indian girl with me or I would have protested, but by the time I had figured it out, Austenaco was long gone.

Her name was Hialeah, which I came to understand later on meant 'beautiful meadow.' She seemed to know right off what needed to be done, and I was grateful for the extra hand. It gave me the opportunity to do a lot more of the chores that needed to be done.

After a couple of months had gone by, Hialeah seemed to be gaining a considerable amount of weight. Finally, the light shown bright, and it dawned on me that she had been with child all along. Over a period of time, Hialeah and I taught each other words and signs, so we could understand each other a right smart better.

Trappers had found her in the woods picking wild berries. They overpowered her and had their way with her. It felt like a ghost had walked over my grave when it came to mind that it might have been the same trappers who had killed my family. When her people found out, Hialeah was disgraced and excluded from the tribe, her family dishonored.

SHORT STACK

Austenaco had brought her to me for two reasons: to give me a helping hand with the twins and to give her and the child she carried a home. With Hialeah looking out for the twins, I was able to do a better job of tending the garden, and I could go hunting when we needed meat. I was able to work the traps proper along the river. Pelts from the beaver I trapped would buy the supplies that were now beginning to run dangerously low. I knew the trip to the trading post was going to be treacherous, but there was no way around it. Before winter set in again, I had to make the journey to the trading post, and I knew I had to do it before Hialeah delivered her baby.

When the season on the mountain began to change, it was beautiful to gaze at the trees along the ridgeline with their colors of gold, red and orange painted against the pale blue Tennessee sky. I kept a careful watch on the season as it changed, and when it was cold enough and the trees had shed their leaves, Austenaco and Hialeah helped me prepare the winter meat, hanging it in the smokehouse to cure. That was a tedious but necessary chore. With that behind me, I knew I had to make the trip to the trading post for the supplies we desperately needed. I had a number of pelts to trade, but I also knew anyone looking at me would think I didn't know what I was doing and they wouldn't want to pay top dollar for my pelts. The actual trading might turn out to be the hardest challenge I had faced so far.

    I packed the supplies I would need for the trip and lit out early the next morning. It was a hard journey. I didn't know it at the time, but Austenaco followed me all the way to the trading post, just to make sure I made it. The men at the settlement gave me a rough time of it like I knew they would, but I stood my ground, and finally I managed fair trade for the supplies we needed. Now, all I had to do was get them back to the cabin. I loaded the pack horse—the coffee, flour, and sugar were not much of a problem, but the calf and baby pig I had purchased sure were a handful. After studying on it a considerable while, I finally carried the baby pig on my lap, and I tied the calf to my horse.

    When I finally started for home, the men at the settlement laughed at me, calling me "Shorty" and "Half Pint." I had Pa's rifle with me, and I let them see it. I had just reached the outskirts of the settlement, and I surely felt relieved and grateful to see Austenaco waving at me. His silhouette on horseback was barely visible in the shadow of the woods. At that moment, I realized just how much I had come to love Austenaco. No matter what I was up against, I knew I did not have to feel alone—Austenaco was a true friend.

The day we reached home and I could first see the cabin, I wanted to cry, but I didn't. Hialeah helped me unload the supplies and then I put the calf and the pig in the small shelter Pa had built for the animals. Pa had called it his shed.

Within a few days of my return, the first snow fell. The same peaceful feeling came over me. I knew the mountain would be too dangerous for anyone to travel. I could settle in with little worry of any outsiders doing us harm. It didn't take long for the twins to get restless and cranky being cooped up in the cabin. I have to admit, with the routine I had come to know, the restless feeling was settling into me, too, inside the walls of the cabin.

Our boredom was broken one afternoon by an unexpected visitor—a dog. Pa hadn't minded if we had a dog, but you had to find one first, seeing as they was about as scarce as hen's teeth. So I knew right off she likely belonged to someone. She was beautiful, a mix of some sort, and I could tell right off she had more than a little wolf in her. I had to wonder about the owner—maybe someone had been trying to climb the mountain, now maybe they was in trouble.

The dog was warming herself by the fire as I loaded Pa's gun. She looked at me with big, sad, brown eyes. It came to mind the dog just might be hungry, so I fed her. When she finished the food I gave her, I heard myself ask out loud, "Is someone out there on the mountain, girl?"

I knew if there was someone out there, they must not have a lick of sense to be crossing the mountain in the middle of winter. I left the cabin with the dog by my side, but I did not want to leave Hialeah alone for any length of time. The baby would be coming soon, and when her time came, I did not want her to go through it all on her lonesome. She was already showing signs of distress in her lower back, and it was getting harder and harder for her to get up and down from Ma's rocker.

Outside in the harsh elements, the dog seemed to know where I needed us to go. The wind was blowing a mite fierce that day, and it was a bitter cold. The snow was deep, and it made the going rough. Whoever had tried to climb up the mountain at this time of year had to be a damn fool.

About a mile and a half north of the cabin, I found him. He had fallen asleep in the snow, probably from exhaustion. He would have frozen to death if I hadn't of found him. He looked right familiar, but I couldn't place where I might have seen him. I couldn't wake him, so I tried dragging him a spell, but I was running out of time and strength. At our rate of travel, he would be dead before I could get him to the cabin.

Finally, I looked through the meager amount of supplies he carried and found a length of rope. I tied the rope off just beneath his arms and then pulled the rope back through to circle each shoulder. I tied the other end of the rope around the dog's shoulders. I positioned myself along the rope, between him and the dog, in order to help the dog pull him. There was no doubt in my mind, if the stranger ever woke up, he would be a mite sore and bruised from being dragged like that, but at least he would be alive to hurt. By the time I reached the cabin I was exhausted, but the stranger was still breathing. I had stopped several times on the way back to rest and check on him.

When I opened the cabin door I saw such a mess, that so help me God, if Pa had been living, he would have skinned those boys alive. The twins were wide awake, and they sat happily in the middle of the floor, playing in the flour barrel they had knocked over. I knew it would have taken the two of them to knock that barrel over. I gave them both a sound licking. I felt bad doing it, but they had to learn.

Hialeah had been helpless against the twins. She was right slap-dab in the midst of having her baby. I needed Pa's strength—I needed Ma's wisdom. I didn't know the first thing about birthing babies. I finally managed to get the stranger into Pa's bed, and then I rushed to check on Hialeah. She was in world of pain, screaming at the top of her lungs in her own language with the terrible swell of each labor pain. It would be a long night. I had to stop for a moment and think the situation over. The cabin was a wreck, Hialeah was having a baby, and I had rescued a stranger, who might be dying.

The way I looked at it, since the dog refused to leave his master's side, the stranger was taken care of, least for the moment. There was little else I could do for him but keep cold, wet clothes on his feverish head, and make sure the rest of him stayed covered up good. There wasn't much else I could do for him, as the fever had him. The fever would have to run its course, one way or the other. If he died in the cabin, I would just have to move him outside, until the ground unfroze enough to bury him. He talked some from the fever, but nothing I could really understand with all of my concentration focused on Hialeah.

About three o'clock that morning, I helped deliver a bouncing baby boy. Hialeah was tired and weak from the ordeal, but otherwise doing fine. Right off, Hialeah wasn't sure what to name her son. If she gave him an Indian name, white folks wouldn't accept him. If she gave him a white man's name, the Indians wouldn't accept him.

Finally, Hialeah decided this new baby was now a part of our family. She gave him our family name of McDaniels and the Cherokee name Adahy, meaning "in the oak woods." Adahy McDaniels became a new addition to our family.

Four days went by before the stranger's fever finally broke. I was relieved to hear him start to stir. After a few moments, I saw his eyelids begin to flutter, and then he opened his eyes. When he began to move his head from side to side to look around, I sat down beside the bed and said, "You been asleep going on three days. I reckon you must be right hungry."

I was walking away from him when he spoke for the first time. "I hope your cooking has improved, Short Stack." I turned to face him, feeling a mite uneasy, as he had known my name.

"Mister, have our paths crossed before?"

He smiled weakly. "Not really, Short Stack. But I know all about you. Your Pa wrote me. I'm David Jo McDaniels, your Pa's brother."

I knew Pa had a brother, but he was supposed to be a fancy lawyer somewhere down around North Carolina. David had grown up on the mountain, and I could accept him being Pa's brother. But it did not explain why he had been foolish—or desperate—enough to attempt crossing the mountain in the middle of winter. I fetched him some soup and sat down next to him.

"What should I call you? David or Uncle David?"

He smiled at me and allowed that David would do just fine. I explained about Hialeah and her new baby, and then I let know him about Pa and the rest of my family. I saw the tears of sorrow well in his eyes, but he didn't cry. Pa would have done the same thing.

"Short Stack, I think you and the twins would be better off coming back down the mountain with me. These mountains are dangerous. You can't raise the boys all alone with no man around."

I know he was trying to do right by us, and Pa would have wanted him to do it, but what he said lit a fire in me. I looked at him with a blaze of grit and determination.

"David, this here mountain is my home. I'm not about to leave it. My Pa is buried just outside this here cabin alongside my Ma and my sisters. My blood is on this mountain, and I don't intend to ever leave it. So far, I've done just fine. So I won't listen to any more talk of leaving this mountain."

David fell silent and ate the soup I gave him. He was just too weak to argue with me. He drifted back to sleep, but I knew in my heart, if he was anything like Pa, he wouldn't give up until I left the mountain.

I sat by the fire watching the flames dance in the fireplace. At least I would have some company until spring, unless David decided to be a damn fool again and try to make it back down the mountain. I really didn't know what David intended to do. The way I looked at it, David had two easy choices. He could stay, or he could leave. After all, he was family, and he was welcome to stay, but if he chose to leave, it would be alone.

There were still unanswered questions concerning David's arrival. He hadn't known Pa had been killed, so why would he suddenly put himself in harm's way by climbing the mountain? Whatever he decided, my mind was made up: I wasn't leaving the mountain. All three boys were going to be raised on this mountain. They would all be mountain men some day, strong and brave enough to go bear hunting with a switch. This land would be passed down to my brothers someday. I would not walk away from their legacy—Pa wouldn't want me to.

CHAPTER 6
Grace of Truth

Early the next morning, I was up before dawn tending to the livestock while my brothers were still sleeping. I didn't mind feeding the animals, but I hated milking old Sassy Pants. Ma used to milk her and I swear that cow was stubborn as a bowed-up old pack mule. She would take offense if'n anybody else but Ma tried milking her. I can remember the first time Ma tried to show me how to milk Sassy Pants. I was sitting on that very same stool trying to milk that very same old cow with no success. I tried warming up my hands, I tried pulling and squeezing those teats just like Ma had showed me, but not one solitary drop of milk. She was kicking and moving around on me. Ma laughed at me until I thought she would split her sides. I got real mad at Ma and stormed off into the woods, and I didn't come back till dinner time. Pa chewed on me for quite a spell over that one. If Ma could see me now, she would be right proud.

By the time I finished up with my morning chores—the milking, feeding the animals and carrying in wood for the fire—I knew the boys would be up and stirring, and they'd be wanting some breakfast, so I hurried back inside the cabin. David was awake, standing by the fireplace. He knew things weren't right between us. The tension had been building, I just couldn't trust David with things the way they stood.

"Morning, David."

He nodded his head slowly and wished me the same. After a few moments of silence, I just came right out with it.

"I have to ask you, David. What brought you all the way up the mountain the middle of winter? That was a right fool thing to do."

He smiled hesitantly and looked away, not looking at me directly in the eye. "Well, Short Stack, it's a long story, but it looks like it's going to be a long winter." He paced the floor in front of the fireplace, seeming to study his stocking feet.

"I was older than your Pa. I arrived by ship a few months after your Pa arrived here on the mountain. I stayed on until we had enough money to bring our folks across the ocean. Our folks never made it to the mountain. We heard tell the vessel went down in a storm, and there were no survivors.

Our Ma had always wanted your Pa and me to learn to read and write. I took to book learning like a duck to water, your Pa not so much. I read everything I could get my hands on, and as I took a notion to become a lawyer, I left the mountain. I really never wanted to be a farmer. Your Pa stayed on the mountain to take care of his family. Your Pa wanted me to come back and help out for a spell after the twins were born, but a year had come and gone by the time I got word. I kept all of his letters and feeling a mite homesick, I felt the need to come back to the mountain. So here I am."

David's story sounded all well enough and good, but it just didn't sit right with me. In truth, I wasn't really satisfied with his explanation for coming back to the mountain. Pa had taught me to look a body in the eye when I was talking. David shifted his eyes around the room when he spoke— he was really never looking at me straight on. There was more to his story, I was sure of it. Nobody in their right mind would have tried to cross the mountain in the middle of winter just because he was feeling a "mite homesick." David had grown up here. He knew the mountain from his younger days. I wanted to pursue the conversation, but the twins were awake, fussing and hungry.

I made breakfast, fed the twins and then got them dressed. After looking out for my brothers, I looked in on Hialeah. She was dressed and sitting in Ma's rocker, holding her new baby boy. I felt right proud to have been there with her when Adahy was born. It didn't matter none to me that Adahy was what some folks called a half-breed. From the moment I held that child in my arms for the first time, I loved him. Thinking back on it, I fell in love with him the first time he cried for life.

I made breakfast for Hialeah and David. I still wasn't much good at cooking, but then again, I had improved some since Ma had died. I always figured that a body was bound to improve with something they do every day, but my pancakes just didn't seem to be one of them. David must have found the pancakes tolerable—maybe he didn't want to hurt my feelings, or maybe anything would have tasted good with his appetite renewed. Either way, he ate every bite.

I couldn't help but wonder about the letters Pa had written to his brother over the years. In my eyes, Pa had been one hell of a man—I loved him dearly—but David had already mentioned Pa had said I wasn't much good at cooking. What else had Pa said about me? After I washed up the morning dishes, and I finally got up the courage to ask.

"David, what else did Pa say about me? Do you have his letters with you?"

David smiled, "Short Stack, he adored you. He

told me you were a quick study and that you knew the mountain like the back of your hand. He swore there was neither varmint nor bird you couldn't mimic. Your Pa knew you loved the mountain as much as he did. He was right proud of you, Short Stack."

I turned toward the cabin window to keep David from seeing the tears in my eyes. My Pa had meant everything to me. He was gone and I missed him something awful. I heard David walk up behind me, but I didn't turn around to face him. I just stood there with my back towards him. There was just something about David that didn't set right with me yet, so I couldn't fully trust him, even if he was family.

"Short Stack, I've been away from the mountain a long time, but if you can put up with me, I'd like to stay on a spell and help out. I know you won't leave the mountain. You're so much like your Pa. I know how to read and write, and I could teach the boys. I brought some books with me, if you would like to read one or two of them. I bet the only book you have ever read is your Ma's Bible."

I turned toward David and smiled, even though I couldn't quite work up the faith to trust him. I hadn't yet needed to put up a fight for the mountain, but I also felt David had given up too easily. That was *not* what Pa would have done.

SHORT STACK

I knew I would have to show David the ways of the mountain he had forgotten. I always believed that living in town doesn't go far in keeping a body strong or the mind sharp. David had to rebuild his strength and endurance. The mountain was beautiful, but treacherous for someone who did not know the hidden dangers beneath that beauty. As I had learned the hard way, on the mountain, a body pays a dear price for a mistake.

Within a couple of weeks, David had recovered enough to start helping me with the chores, and I was grateful for the extra hand. He worked hard doing chores around the cabin, always looking for something else to do. At times, I felt funny thinking I should have had stronger feelings for him, especially when he was working so hard, but all I knew of him was bits and pieces, of David's own stories and some of Pa's childhood memories. In some ways he resembled Pa—he was tall and handsome. His hair was the color of spun sand and his eyes were a deep brown, but no matter how much David looked like Pa, no one could ever replace my Pa, or even begin to fill his shoes.

The twins, Adahy and Hialeah got along just fine with David. He had a gentle patience with them. Hialeah had started making clothes for the boys from a bolt of cloth I had brought back from the trading post. She had a real knack for sewing, which made me right happy, as I wasn't much good at it. Hialeah would sit in Ma's rocker sewing and singing the songs of her people. Most of the time, I didn't understand the words, but her voice was beautiful and soothing. Come to think of it, she had a song to sing with almost any chore she did, and it was surely agreeable listening.

Winter had started to pass, and the snow was beginning to melt from the mountain. David was growing restless like a bug on a hot rock in the middle of July. I was waiting for the right moment to speak with David, alone. That night after supper, David and I was playing checkers in front of the fireplace. He was a right smart checker player. He never let me win, but that night he did. His mind was not focused on playing checkers. I waited for the boys and Hialeah to fall asleep before I tried to talk to David. Finally, after the checkers had been put away, we sat at the kitchen table drinking a cup of coffee, but David was staring out at nothing.

I softly touched his arm and said, "David, I know something is eating away at you. Whatever it is, I want to be able to deal with it when the time comes. If you don't want my help, at least tell me it won't put us in any danger."

He looked at me for a long moment, his deep brown eyes searching mine. I realized he was about to tell me the truth. For once, David was looking me straight in the eye.

"Short Stack, I don't rightly know where to begin. But believe me, I'm sorry I just couldn't tell you when I first came back up the mountain. I was ashamed, you see, because I never actually became a lawyer. Oh, I studied all right and could have made a fine lawyer, but I took up some bad habits after I left the mountain—gambling, chasing women and drinking. I forgot the promise I made to my folks. I was wild and reckless with my life. I fell in love with the wrong sort of woman. I knew deep down she was no good, but I loved her. I caught her with another man, and he pulled a gun on me, but I fired first. I had no choice Short Stack, I killed him. I've been running ever since. I knew the mountain would be dangerous to cross, but I had to take the chance. Now, there's a good chance men will come looking for me. If you want me to move on, I will. I don't want to bring down no trouble on you."

I was shocked, but I felt like it took a lot of guts for him to tell me the truth, and I believed him to be sincere. If there was any bad seed left in David, I hadn't seen it. When I looked into his eyes, I saw only kindness and a penitent spirit.

"David, if trouble comes, we will just have to ford that stream when we come to it. You done right by me, and I won't turn my back on you because you're in trouble. Try not to fret too much over this. Maybe no one will even come looking for you. After all, who would have thought you had a chance of ever making it across the mountain in the middle of winter anyhow?"

David smiled at me as I started to get up from the table, and I smiled right back at him. I felt relieved that he had seen fit to confide in me and grace me with the truth. Now, I believed I could trust him.

"I got myself a bad itch to go hunting in the morning. If'n you're a mind to go, I'll be up by first light, David."

CHAPTER 7
Day of Judgment

Some of the trees on the mountain were beginning to bud, and others were already showing blossoms: the maple, cedar, chestnut, cottonwood, hickory, the white and yellow pine, the oak, elm, and walnut. Pa taught me to recognize most every kind of tree on the mountain. All of them were beautiful, and their blossoms were a welcome sight. The grass was turning green, and the birds were building their nests, butterflies fluttered over the wildflowers dancing with the honeybees. The rich aroma of the Tennessee earth softly scented the air. Spring had found its way once again to the mountain.

The twins were now five years old. Most people would have thought twin brothers would be double trouble, but my brothers always seemed to keep each other occupied, amusing each other to no end. They were identical twins, and it was hard for anyone except me looking at the boys to know which one was Clayton and which one was Catlin. I was there when they were born, and Ma had showed me how. I knew Catlin had a small birthmark on the left side of his head. The birthmark was a light color of pink and it bordered on his hairline. Unless you knew where to look, you would never know the mark was there. If I ever had a doubt in my mind, I looked.

Hialeah kept good watch over the young'uns and did the cooking while David and I hunted, tended the garden and ran the traplines along the river. David's dog, Cleo was a good protector while we were away from the cabin, and soon the boys and Cleo were inseparable. She was part wolf and had a good instinct about her. Cleo could be one mean dog to tangle with, if'n she believed you were going to hurt one of the boys, or any of us for that matter.

David was proving himself to be quite a mountain man. I don't believe David ever realized he was capable of doing it. There was a lot of good in David. He was a gentle, quiet man who worked from sun up to sun down then at night he'd sit by the fireplace, reading poetry to the children. With each passing day, I found it harder and harder to believe David had killed anyone. His heart and soul had returned to the mountain, but his body was wanted for murder.

The Day of Judgment descended on David the first part of June. David and I were running the traplines along the river, when I noticed the clouds of dust being kicked up and felt the pounding hooves of the soldiers' horses as they rumbled the ground beneath my feet. I knew it wasn't very likely that much dust was being kicked up by Indians since they didn't want anyone to see them coming. Common sense told me soldiers, and it gave me a sick feeling in the pit of my stomach, as soldiers could be looking for David.

My harsh whisper was desperate. "David, get back to the cabin and stay put, until I tell you to come out!" He seemed frozen in place, so I picked up a small stone close to me. I squalled with everything I had and threw the stone as hard as I could. When the stone bounced off the side of his face, he came back to life and stared at me. "David, get a move on! The soldiers are coming this way. Go! Now!"

At first, David did exactly what I asked him to do. Both of us hurried toward the cabin, and I stayed outside, pretending I was tending to the garden. I stood in full view of the approaching soldiers. The ground shuddered underneath my feet, and my heart seemed to beat a little faster with each hoof that hit the ground.

A young lieutenant leading the soldiers held up his hand, motioning the soldiers behind him to stop with his signal. He feigned a long stretch in the saddle, looking the cabin over before he climbed down from his horse. He wasn't really clever about it—anyone would have known what he was doing. Cleo was standing alongside of me, and she just didn't cotton to this lieutenant walking toward me. She walked right in between us, releasing a low growl of warning. The young lieutenant smiled halfheartedly as he stopped real sudden-like and tipped his hat to me.

"Miss, my name is Lieutenant Michael Walker and we are looking for a man wanted for murder. His name is David Jo McDaniels. I understand you are some kin to him."

I had never been much good at lying. I was stuttering, trying to think up just the right thing to say to the young lieutenant. When the cabin door suddenly swung wide open, David stepped boldly outside and faced Michael Walker.

"Good afternoon, gentlemen. What can I do for you?"

I realized in less than a heartbeat what he was about to do. He didn't want anyone to get hurt for something he had done. David was going to tell Lieutenant Michael Walker the truth. I felt the panic welling up inside me. He would hang for sure

SHORT STACK

if he turned himself over to the soldiers, but Pa's words came to mind.

I was eight years old, and I was angry with Pa for making me do something I really didn't want to do. I guess I had it coming for sassing him, but my sister Kimberly had started it. She talked me into doing her chores by promising to help Ma with the dishes that night. After supper, Kimberly Ann suddenly forgot her promise. I was arguing up a storm with Kimberly and Ma, when Pa stepped in and told me to help Ma do the dishes. I tried to explain, but Pa gave me a long, hard look which commanded silence. I was mad as a wet hen, but I knew Pa would give me a licking if I argued with him. I helped Ma with the dishes, but every chance I got, when Pa wasn't looking, I stuck my tongue out at Kimberly. After the dishes were done, I walked outside the cabin into the warmth of a lazy summer night. The wind dried my tears as fast as they fell. I felt hurt and severely wronged. Pa gave me a couple of minutes to think everything over, and then he followed me outside.

"Short Stack, there will be moments in your life—just like tonight—that really won't seem fair, but life isn't always fair. Sometimes you're going to have to face hard choices—life is full of them. But if you believe in your heart you have made the right choice then Short Stack, don't ever switch your horses in midstream."

Pa's wisdom from the past helped me make a painful decision. Whether it was the right choice or whether it was the wrong choice, I would have to stand by the decision I made that day.

I spoke up before David could say another word. "Pa, these men are looking for your brother, David. I was just fixing to tell them where he was."

Lieutenant Walker now focused his attention on me, so I continued with an ease I really didn't feel.

"Lieutenant, David McDaniels is buried right here alongside my sisters and my Ma. Trappers killed my Ma and sisters near two years back. I found David on the mountain this past winter. Damn fool should have known better than to try and cross this here mountain in the dead of winter. He was froze solid to an elm tree. I can show you where I found him if'n you're a mind to see."

The young lieutenant looked at me long and hard. I shifted my weight from one leg to the other, just like I would have done if Pa had been scolding me for something. I had never been much good at telling tales, and for a long moment there, I thought the young lieutenant wasn't going to believe my story. The lieutenant's stern look suddenly averted to the cabin door, as the twins ran from inside the cabin, beating fast tracks for David. Looking back, I can admit at the time it hurt my feelings something fierce. I had taken care of my brothers after the death of our folks, but when they sensed danger, they ran for David. Michael Walker looked at the twins and then gave David a long hard look. The twins looked so much like Pa and so did David. After several moments of fearful silence, the young lieutenant tipped his hat.

"I'm sorry to have disturbed you good folks. I will report my findings to the proper authorities. We will camp down by the river tonight. If you require any further assistance, please do not hesitate to ask."

I smiled innocently at Lieutenant Walker and said, "I saw some deer on the south ridge of the mountain this morning if you're in need of some fresh meat." I stood there in front of the cabin until the soldiers disappeared from sight.

I turned and looked at David with fire in my eyes, and I didn't even try to hide the anger I felt. I know he must have felt downright confused to see the resentment in my eyes.

I screamed at David with hot embers simmering in my eyes, my dark brown eyes ready to cast lightning bolts at him. "Watch over the cabin! I'm going to the woods."

I walked through the woods a spell, but I ended up by Pa's grave, crying my eyes out with painful sobs of grief. In my heart no one could have ever replace my Pa, for I loved him dearly. I had saved David's life, but at the same time, I felt deep in my soul I had betrayed my Pa. The same way I felt my brothers had betrayed me by running to David instead of me. Angry tears stormed down my face, a raging torrent I could not control.

I was sitting there feeling sorry for myself, when I felt a gentle hand on my shoulder. It was Austenaco. He did not understand my sadness, but he held me in his arms against his warm, bare chest until I stopped crying. I had not heard his footsteps. I had not sensed danger. That was the last time I ever cried for my Pa. I would love my Ma and Pa forever, and I knew they had loved me, even though now they were gone.

David never mentioned the soldiers to me again or young Lieutenant Michael Walker. There was no need to ever discuss it. He knew how difficult it had been for me to give him Pa's identity. David Jo McDaniels was then known as Jethro McDaniels and from that day forward, it seemed to me David did everything within his power to deserve his brother's name.

Sometimes it hurt my feelings to hear the twins call him Pa. It hurt more than I ever let anyone know. I felt the torment in my soul, but the twins were too young to understand the situation. Someday my brothers would be old enough to

SHORT STACK

understand that David was a good man, but he wasn't Pa. I guess that was the main reason I started correcting the twins whenever they called me Ma, insisting they call me Short Stack. I wanted my brothers to know—to really *know*, when they were old enough to understand—what our folks were like. I wanted them to know I was their sister, not their Ma. I needed to share with them all of the memories I held in my heart of our Ma and Pa.

I also believed in my heart David must have felt blind-sided and gut-kicked about everything. It had happened so quickly, but at the same time, I also felt David should have known how difficult it was for me. I did what I had to do, even though after all was said and done, I didn't cotton to it at all. I didn't switch horses in mid-stream, and I had to believe Pa would have done the same thing.

CHAPTER 8
Evil Spirits

Autumn was descending on the mountain. The beautiful colors of fall decorated the trees with colors of gold, light burgundy, red-yellow, and orange. David and I were out every day running the traplines for beaver. Autumn's early morning hours were crisp and cool on the mountain, until about mid-morning, when the sun climbed higher in the Tennessee sky. Then the wildlife of the mountain would come out to scamper through the autumn leaves, enjoying the last glistening rays of the summer sun.

The days were steadily growing cooler each day. It was plain as the nose on my face, I would have to make the trip to Warner's Trading Post, and I would have to do it soon before the first snowfall. The brisk autumn wind was telling me I couldn't wait much longer to begin my journey.

I knew David could not take the chance of

going to the trading post. Folks who knew Pa just might mosey into the trading post. What if someone by chance noticed the man trading pelts as Jethro McDaniels was indeed not that man? But then again Ole Man Warner didn't seem to miss Pa coming to the trading post, as nobody had ever come looking for my Pa. I also knew without a doubt, David would not want me going alone, and he would likely put up a big fuss—well, I would just have to cross that bridge when I came to it. I really wasn't looking forward to the trip, but it had to be done.

David had returned to the mountain, and it seemed he had found the life he wanted. He watched out for all of us and took on that responsibility with no complaints. The home he had once been so determined to leave now brought him peace, except for the night I told him I was going to the trading post, and he had to stay put.

The twins were walking and talking by then. It seemed like nothing ever slowed them down. Every spare minute I could find, I had them out in the woods. I wanted them to be comfortable there. I wanted to show them every inch of the mountain. When Adahy was old enough, my brothers and I would teach him, too.

Little Adahy was growing fast and always seemed to be happy and content. Hialeah was an instinctive mother—loving but firm with all three boys. She was so beautiful, and I thought it was a downright shame that Hialeah had been cast out by her own people. I always believed kinfolk was supposed to watch out for each other and stand together as one in a fight.

Sometimes, I had a real hard time understanding the Cherokee. One of their own squaws would be allowed to marry a prosperous white man, who might gift the father of the bride with horses, trinkets and blankets. And yet they would disown an innocent girl like Hialeah, who—through no fault of her own—had been wronged so appallingly. This made no sense to me at all. 'Pon my honor, if'n it had been me instead of Hialeah, my Pa would have hunted those bastards down like dogs and made them pay dearly for hurting me.

I always felt Austenaco was a little sweet on Hialeah, but he never let his true feelings show. Every once in awhile, when he left fresh meat for us, there would be some small trinket or a string of beads left for Hialeah. For her however, it was the other way around. Whenever she looked at Austenaco, her eyes melted around him. There was no shadow of a doubt how she felt about him. It had been a good spell since we had seen Austenaco, and I was beginning to worry about him some. But it always seemed like whenever I needed

Austenaco, he showed up right on time.

A couple of days later, we met up down by the river, while I was checking and setting traps. I had been waiting on David to return with the bear fat I needed to grease up the traps. When I heard a twig suddenly snap behind me, I broke one of Pa's strictest rules.

"Keep your eyes and ears open girl—no telling what sort of mountain varmint could be sneaking up on you. Don't ever take nothin' for granted."

In the back of my mind, I figured it was David returning with the bear fat and never paid the snapping twig any mind, until it was too late.

It was a small hunting party, consisting of four Kiowa braves. As I was to find out later, they were a well-known and bitter enemy of the Cherokee. The braves had been watching me for a right smart while. Clearly, I had not been listening to the warning signs around me. Now, I'm not making excuses, but I wasn't expecting to meet up with any Indian who wanted my long auburn hair to hang from his lance, or on a pole in front of his teepee lodge.

I was pulling a beaver from a trap by the river's edge, and so intent at the task at hand that I was unaware of the hands of hate until they gripped my throat. Pa would have been real disappointed in me, for I wasn't even able to reach my gun. I tried to fight, but there was nothing I could do. I had been careless, despite having been taught even as a young'un that such foolishness just might cost me my life.

Austenaco had been following the Kiowa. He had not been real concerned until the Indian braves up and stumbled onto me. The whites were forcing many of the Indian tribes from their hunting grounds—the Chickasaw, the Choctaw, the Creek, the Seminole and the Kiowa were all scrambling to find meat. Austenaco knew the braves were hunting the woods to find food, and even though the two tribes were enemies, they had become like passing shadows in the night, each tribe circling the other, stalking one another with neither sound nor fury.

Unless push came to shove, the Cherokee and the Kiowa shared the hunting grounds. Their common enemy now was the white man, who had pushed them farther into the hills of Tennessee and North Carolina.

Austenaco quickly fired his long rifle into the air. The white wispy smoke circled in the air above his rifle. In less than a blink of an eye, the attention of the Kiowa braves was now focused on Austenaco. I could feel the cold steel blade of a knife pressing against my throat as I strained to see Austenaco. Even if he had been startled by Austenaco's rifle fire, the Kiowa brave holding the knife at my throat never loosened his grip on me. The sweat of my brow was trickling down the side of my face. Austenaco screamed with a thunderous voice at the Kiowa braves. I had not understood one single word he had spoken, but whatever was said, the young brave who had hold of me gave me a very strange look. It was the sort of look you might give someone if you thought they were crazy, or a brick or two short of a full load.

It was at that moment David walked into the small clearing. He walked right into the middle of it. Austenaco screamed at David, raising his arm high into the air holding his rifle above his head, motioning for him to stop. You better believe he stopped dead in his tracks. I suddenly had an idea come to mind. The young brave holding the knife at my throat, had told me something with his eyes. Pa's words echoed in my mind.

"Watch a person's eyes, Short Stack. You can tell what a body is thinking if you just watch their eyes. You can see if someone is happy or sad. You can see if they're hiding something or being honest. It shines in the eyes, Short Stack."

Austenaco must have been trying to convince the Indian brave I was bewitched or crazy. He was moving his finger in a whirlpool motion alongside his head, making funny faces. If the Indians believed you were crazy, they would not harm you.

It was their belief that the evil spirits who made you crazy might be released, and they would come to possess another body, and they surely didn't want it to be them.

With all the might I could muster, I jerked free of the young brave. I shook my finger close to his face just like I had seen Ma do so many times when I was getting scolded. I looked at him with angry eyes and hollered at him, with my hands on my hips.

"How many times do I have to tell you? I don't like you boys running around in the woods playing with knives—why a body could get hurt!"

I reached out with one quick motion, grabbed the knife from his hand and threw it to the ground, never changing the tone of my voice.

"If you and your friends want to play in these woods, you have to be more careful." I smiled wickedly at the young brave and swatted him hard on the backside.

"Now, you boys run off and play. I've got work to do here."

Austenaco had my back, and he translated every word to the Kiowa. I walked away from the young Indian braves and finished taking the beaver from my trap. When I glanced up at the young brave, who could have easily killed me, I saw real fear in his eyes. I was just as fearful of him, but I couldn't let him see it. I felt downright thankful that I had not wet myself.

It didn't take him no time at all to decide that I was touched by evil spirits. The Kiowa braves did not want to take a chance on my sanity, and they did not waste any time with their departure.

After the Kiowa hunting party had cleared the ridge, Austenaco and David couldn't contain their laughter and neither could I. Austenaco was rotating his hand in a spiral gesture of mirth by the side of his head, making funny faces at me, and then he shook his finger in my face just like I had done to the Kiowa brave.

When the laughter had passed, David wiped the tears from his eyes and said, "Short Stack, we better get these here traps up to the cabin. The night shadows are beginning to fall."

I looked at Austenaco standing there with a smile on his face that told me I had a real friend. I walked straight up to him, put my arms around his neck, and as I held him close, I whispered, "Thank you, my friend."

Austenaco seemed surprised, but said nothing. When I let go of him, there was an awkward moment, but then David broke the silence with laughter in his voice and a twinkle of mischief in his eyes.

"When I was at the cabin, Hialeah was a making

up some mighty fine venison stew, with some mouth-watering biscuits. Those vittles should be just about done. I don't think she would mind us a bringing back another mouth to feed, but we best get a move on. We best load up these traps and get back up to the cabin."

When we reached the cabin, the sweet aroma of venison drifted through the air before we even opened the cabin door. There was also freshly baked blackberry pies cooling on the table. Hialeah was indeed very pleased when Austenaco joined us for supper that night. The brilliance of her eyes told a story of true love. A foolish folly of love that could never be, but it didn't matter. Hialeah would cherish each moment when her eyes could see his soul.

CHAPTER 9
The Mountain Man

It was mid-October by the time I set out for the trading post with Austenaco. It had not been an easy decision for David to let me go without him, but with Austenaco along for the ride, the journey would be easier and safer for me. I was more than a little skittish about this trip, but I never let on. I knew I would be carrying a lot more pelts this time. I had to make sure those pelts reached the trading post to trade for the supplies we needed or we would most likely not survive the winter. I felt the weight on my shoulders, and I didn't cotton to it, but there was no way around it.

The second night of the trip, Austenaco and I camped in a small clearing shrouded by oak and elm trees. The stars in the Tennessee sky shined like diamonds, adorning a harvest moon full and bright. The campfire took the edge off the crisp night air. We were tired and hungry from the day's riding. The black coffee warmed our tired bones, and the dried beef satisfied our hunger.

Austenaco and I were settling in for the night, when we heard the horses. We looked at each other at the same time. I grabbed my rifle. Austenaco disappeared into the woods, quiet as a shadow. I sat there by the fire with fear eating at me, not knowing what was about to ride up on us. When the horses finally rode into camp, the fear vanished like a thief in the night. It was replaced with pure hate. I was all of a sudden looking at the four men who had killed my family. I took careful aim at the man who I saw with my own eyes drag my Ma into our cabin. He was also the ugly bastard who had dangled Ma's gold locket in his hands—so proud of his plundered treasure.

In my mind, I was reliving that awful night. It was something I can't even explain or begin to understand, then or now. My mind just wasn't working proper, but the instinct for survival took over. I had one advantage—they had never laid eyes on me. They had no idea who this young girl was that they'd happened upon alone in the woods. Hate danced in my eyes, alongside the reflected blistering flames of the campfire. I scrambled to my feet with my rifle in my hand. I never lowered my gun. I kept it cocked and aimed at the one I so desperately wanted to kill. I could tell they were sizing up the camp they'd stumbled across and me as well. It was so easy to read their thoughts: *easy pickin's*.

After a minute or two, the big ugly bastard stretched in his saddle easy-like and then finally spoke right up. "Little lady, you shouldn't be out here all by your lonesome. Where's the menfolk? These here woods can be downright dangerous."

He started to get down from his horse. My face burned with the fire of revenge fed by the poisonous fuel of hatred.

"Don't you bother getting down off'n your horse, or 'pon my honor, you'll be on your way to hell before your feet touch the ground!"

He smiled wickedly at me, only hesitating a moment before he started to climb down from his horse, daring me to fire. I obliged him. I wanted to kill him, and I could have, but there were four of them to handle. The shot I fired knocked him from his horse and spun him in a circle before he hit the ground. The other three men looked at me with surprise in their eyes as they scrambled for cover.

I jumped behind the closest tree and screamed, "Get the hell out of here! The menfolk are sure to be making fast tracks for me now. That shot was easy heard for a country mile."

It come clear to me pretty quick that none of them were of a mind to take me serious enough.

Once the wounded trapper made it to the cover of the trees, they all opened fire. They were bold, believing I couldn't shoot straight enough to defend myself. In one of the dumbest moves I ever saw, the first one ran straight for me. I took careful aim and fired. The trader was dead before he hit the ground. Within a split second of his scream, I heard another.

Austenaco fired at one of the men making his move on me while I was trying to reload my rifle. Listening to the sounds of the night around me, I took deep breaths waiting for someone to try something. I heard one last shot fired and some scuffling and then the night fell silent. It was several minutes before I heard the hooves of two horses pounding the earth in a hurried flight. When it was all over, two of the trappers lay dead, and one of the two who had rode away was wounded.

I searched the edge of the woods for Austenaco, but he was nowhere to be seen. I waited several minutes, praying to God for him to return safe to the campfire. After it was all over, I trembled a good sight more from fear rather than from the freezing night air. When Austenaco did not return, I became worried. I had to search for him—he might have been hurt. I made sure the two trappers lying within a couple of yards of our campfire were sure enough dead, and then I set out to find Austenaco.

SHORT STACK

The sun was rising in the sky when I finally found Austenaco. My heart began to sink into the sorrow of a deep, cold river of grief when I first spied his still form. I could not see his long, black hair, but once I had rolled him over to face me, I saw his noble expression staring up at the sky. Austenaco was dead. The trappers who had killed Austenaco had also scalped him, taking his long black hair.

I screamed with a broken heart, I screamed with terror.

"God…God...No!"

"God…God…Can't you hear me?"

"Damn it, God! Are you really there?"

Austenaco had been my dearest friend. He had saved my hide more than once. My screams echoed off the mountain, and I didn't care whether man or beast heard me. I knew I could not—would not—leave him in such a shape. Somehow, I had to get him back to his people. The Cherokee had their own kind of burial. At the very least, I owed this to my loyal friend. I would have to backtrack a day's journey, but in my heart and soul, I knew I had no choice. I couldn't stand to look at my friend without the long mantle of hair he'd been so proud of, so I wrapped a cloth around his head where his hair had been.

Dragging my heavy heart and a tired body, I

made my way back to camp and loaded the horses. It took me the better part of an hour to get Austenaco wrapped in a blanket and situated crosswise over his horse. I rode the whole day in silence, emotions roiling inside me like somebody churning fresh butter. Usually, I would just up and speak to Pa like he could hear me and talk it out, but this time, I just couldn't.

I was tired and emotionally spent by the time I reached Austenaco's people. The thought never crossed my mind that his people might actually think I had killed Austenaco. When I rode in with him, I felt the eyes of hate rake over me like the claws of an old horned owl. More than a dozen braves walked up to me with angry eyes fixed solidly on me. I had Pa's rifle cradled in my arms. One of the braves walked up to Austenaco's horse with a fierce stride and pulled my friend down harshly. He then turned toward me and screamed something I didn't understand, but the young Indian braves standing solemnly around me understood exactly what he said. In less than a blink of an eye, I was pulled down from my horse and lying face down on the ground, without Pa's rifle.

I was exhausted and broken-hearted, and I was taken off-guard, stunned by this sudden turn of events. Just when I figured all was lost, and I had no more will to fight, a handsome, rugged looking mountain man stepped into the circle of Indians, who reluctantly surrendered me. His hair was a sandy brown color with golden highlights. His eyes were the deepest brown I had ever seen. He spoke sternly and with authority.

"Girl, tell me what happened."

I gathered my legs beneath me, and I struggled to my feet. I carefully looked that mountain man over before I began to speak.

"Austenaco and I were on our way to Warner's Trading Post. Austenaco came with me to make sure I made it to the trading post with my pelts to trade for supplies. We had a run-in with four trappers—they were the same men who killed my folks and two sisters a couple of years back. Two of the trappers are dead. The other two got away, but one of them is wounded. When Austenaco didn't come back to camp after the fightin' was over, I went looking for him and found him dead. Austenaco was my friend. Twice Austenaco saved my life. I have done what I felt Austenaco would have wanted me to do—bring him back to his people."

The mountain man turned and translated my words. The expressions of the faces around me slowly began to change. A solemn-looking warrior of older years walked up to me. His face was worn and lined with age, but still rugged. He placed a hand on my shoulder and softly whispered, "Short Stack."

I could clearly see my friend in the lines of the warrior's aged face. It made me feel a mite better to know Austenaco had spoken of me.

A squaw bowing her head so shyly walked up to me and took my hand, motioning for me to come with her. The mountain man smiled at me.

"Go with her, Short Stack. She will give you something to eat and show you where you can lie down for a spell and sleep. I'll take these pelts into Ole Man Warner's Trading Post for you and pick up your supplies. Just tell me what you need."

Despite my heart-ache, my exhaustion, and the terror of nearly being killed twice in as many days, I was suddenly madder than an old wet hen! I was furious! This feller wasn't asking my *permission* to go to the trading post with my pelts, he was *telling* me, like I didn't have a choice. I did not return his smile.

"I can go after my own supplies."

He turned sharply around to face me with a look of pure arrogance on his face.

"Now look, Short Stack. I know you got some grit in your gizzard, but the first snow is already blowing in the wind. I can travel faster than you. I'm stronger and I can probably get more money for your pelts than you can, which in turn will give you more supplies."

My temper was burning out of control. "Look, Mountain Man—or whoever you are."

Tipping his big hat with a wicked smile on his face, he quickly interrupted. "Joseph Walker, ma'am. Most folks in these parts call me Joe."

Being emotionally spent, tired, hungry and now mad as hell, I rambled on. "Look, Walker, those are my pelts and it's my family sitting back at the cabin depending on me to bring back those supplies. I don't know you from a hole in the ground. I will go after my own supplies!"

Joe Walker laughed at me as he walked away. I started to pick up the nearest thing to me, which happened to be the unburned end of a log in the fire. I wanted desperately to throw it at him, but after looking quickly around me at the Indians standing close by, I decided against it. Reluctantly, I followed the young Indian girl. I ate the food she offered me and I fell asleep from exhaustion. When I awoke my pelts was gone and so was Joe Walker.

CHAPTER 10
Trouble on the Mountain

I was as jittery as a moth circling a dying flame as I impatiently waited for three long days to see Joe Walker ride back into the Cherokee camp. I couldn't believe the arrogance and confidence of that man. When he finally sauntered into the Indian village on horseback, it infuriated me even more seeing that he had fared much better at the trading post than I ever could have done. The packhorse behind him was overloaded with supplies. He had clearly accomplished what he had set out to do, and it did not matter what I thought about it. I know he meant well, and that was all well and good, but the fact of the matter was, I had not asked for his help.

When he stepped down from his horse, I exploded furiously. "Who the hell gave you permission to trade my pelts, Mr. Walker?" I became even more angry when a broad grin flashed across his handsome face.

"Well, Short Stack, you have to admit, you were pretty exhausted from your ordeal with the trappers. The first snow was in the wind, and someone had to go, so I volunteered. I gave you my help whether you asked for it or not. Oh, and by the way, my little Missy, I purchased a right pretty dress for you while I was there."

Now, I was seething. "Don't you *dare* call me Missy! I can't believe you wasted my pelts on a dress! Where the hell would I wear it? Tending to the garden? Hunting in the woods? Walker, I want you to know that I purely resent you sticking your nose in where it doesn't belong! Now, if you will excuse me, *Mister* Walker, I have to get back home before the first snow."

The smile slowly faded from his face and his mood turned solemn.

"Not without me, Short Stack. Those trappers you tangled with are not likely to forget about you anytime soon. I did some poking around at the trading post and found out those men are wanted by the law. They are dangerous, and I don't reckon they took kindly to you shooting two of 'em dead and wounding another. Varmints like that just multiply—for every man you took out, they will surely add two. It is my duty-bound intention to escort you back to your homestead."

I stared at Joe Walker for several moments,

thinking everything over. I wanted to sleep in my own bed, I wanted to see my brothers, and I wanted to go home. I realized even if I didn't like the situation, I knew he was right—it would be safer to have him along. I also knew it was useless to argue with him. Even if I didn't like the situation, I had to give into good ole common sense. It didn't matter a lick how I felt about things, others were depending on me.

"All right, Walker. But once we reach the cabin I'll provide you with a hot meal, a good night's sleep, and then Mister Walker, we say goodbye."

Who could tolerate a man like that? He walked away from me shrugging his shoulders like he could have cared less about what I thought of him. His laughter ruffled my feathers as he called out over his shoulder, "You're welcome, Short Stack."

By first light, Joe and I began our journey back to the cabin. As I rode toward home, I contemplated having to tell David and Hialeah about Austenaco. I knew Hialeah would take it bad, her heart belonged him. I had always known Austenaco and Hialeah loved each other, but the bond of loyalty to their tribal customs and beliefs had kept them apart. I think it bothered me even more to know that I had to somehow face my brothers and break the terrible news of his death. The boys had been too young to remember the deaths of our family. Now they were old enough to ask questions that would require serious answers. I would have to answer with truth, but in such a way a child could understand. Austenaco had been fond of the twins from the very beginning. He had taught them more of the Cherokee language than I knew. I dreaded the thought of facing my brothers with the story of heaven for Austenaco.

The sun was slowly fading from the sky when Walker and I began to look for a place to camp for the night. Walker decided we should camp in the thick of the woods, instead of a clearing. After I had tied off the horses, I started gathering firewood, but Walker insisted there would be no campfire. If those trappers were about, a fire would draw them to us like moths to a flame. I knew he was right, but I didn't have to like it.

I didn't get much sleep that night. I tossed and turned, but at least I rested some. Every sound coming from the woods caught my attention and echoed through my mind. Two of the trappers were still alive—I knew deep in my heart I could not rest until they were both dead. They had gotten a good look at me, and I knew as sure as night follows day, we would cross paths again and someone would die.

The following night as we rode up to the cabin, the twins bolted through the front door of the cabin with screams and giggles of delight. David and Hialeah were not far behind them. I introduced Joe Walker as we were unloading the supplies.

Hialeah placed her hand on my shoulder and with a smile on her lips, she asked, "Austenaco?"

I took her back inside the cabin before I told her what had happened to him. I never told her they scalped him—Austenaco was gone, and that was hurt enough for her to deal with. She sobbed against my shoulder as I held her close. I had already walked a mile in her moccasins through the gates of hell.

By this time, I was feeling a mite stupid over the way I had treated Joe Walker. I hadn't spoken a civil word to him since the first moment I had laid eyes on him. Whether I cottoned to it or not, I was going to have to thank him before he moved on. I knew it was the proper thing to do, so after supper when everyone had settled in for the night, I spoke to him when the moment presented itself.

"Walker, I have given you a hot meal as promised, and you can roll out a blanket close by the fire."

Walker leaned back in his chair, and flashed a mocking smile at me. "I know, Short Stack. I'll be gone by first light."

I was beginning to feel real flustered. Nothing I said seemed to come out right. "Walker, before you go, I should thank you for everything you've done to help me."

He was still smiling at me, and I was getting irritated again. "Please, call me Joe."

I stood up from the table a little quicker than I really meant to, staring at the mocking smile on his face. "How about you remind me in the morning, Mr. Walker? I'm just too plumb wore out to thank you proper tonight!"

His laughter bellowed behind me as I stormed out of the room. I had an almost uncontrollable urge to throw something at him and make it really hurt. It would have made me feel so much better to lash out at him just once, but I refrained from doing so.

The next morning when my eyes finally opened, the sun was already high in sky. I stretched, yawned, rubbed my eyes, and then I got out of bed. David was sitting at the kitchen table, drinking a cup of coffee.

"Morning, David. Why didn't you wake me for morning chores?"

David smiled at me. "Well, you just got back from a long trip, and I figured you deserved to sleep in a spell. Sit down, I will fix you up a cup of coffee and some vittles, if'n you want some breakfast."

I couldn't help but notice Hialeah was hurting

something awful over Austenaco, but I knew I had to let her grieve in her own way. She was sitting in Ma's rocker sewing, but she wasn't singing. There was never a time that I could remember Hialeah sitting in Ma's rocker with her sewing and *not* singing the songs of her people. I missed her sweet voice, but I knew she needed time and healing.

Looking around the cabin, I knew Joe Walker was gone. I didn't really know how I felt about him being gone. Joe had helped me, and I should have been more tolerant of him, but he was a downright infuriating man. Walker had a laid back way of doing things, and nothing seemed to ruffle his feathers.

Snow was falling in earnest now on the mountain, and I thought of Joe Walker making his crossing. I hoped wherever he was headed that he reached his destination before the snow got too deep. When I thought about it, I didn't know a whole lot about Joe Walker. I didn't know where he was from or where he was going.

I didn't understand why I kept thinking about Walker from time to time. One afternoon, I closed my bedroom door and pulled out a box from under my bed. Inside the box was the dress Joe Walker had purchased for me at the trading post. It was a lovely shade of pink, trimmed in burgundy. The material was soft to the touch. I gave some thought to making some curtains from that dress, but I just never got around to it.

I could relax a little more with the isolation of each snowfall. The mountain was becoming impossible to travel once more. If the trappers took a notion to come after me with the onset of winter, they would surely have a hard go of it.

The twins were growing big enough to start helping me do little chores around the cabin. Every morning they would argue about which one was going to help me with the animals, and I would wind up taking them both. The twins would soon be seven. I decided to teach them how to shoot once spring came back around. Pa had taught me when I was seven, and I figured it was high time the boys learned too. If they fared well, next fall I would buy them their first rifles.

Adahy was crawling by then, and pulling himself up onto just about everything. He would be walking by spring. All three boys knew the language of the Cherokee—Hialeah and Austenaco had taught them. I thought about Austenaco more than I spoke of him, and I dearly missed my friend. I felt partly to blame for his death, and I was having a hard time getting over it. After all, he wouldn't have been out on the mountain if'n it weren't for me.

Every day after the chores had all been taking

SHORT STACK

care of, David commenced to teaching Clayton and Catlin how to read and write. They didn't like sitting still for learning, but it was for their own good. Ma had taught me, and as I recall, I just didn't cotton to it either. I remember one time, when I was supposed to be doing my book learning, I sneaked out of the cabin and went playing in the woods. Ma came after me with a green switch in her hands, but I hid up in the woods. Ma got real mad when she couldn't find me. I waited until Pa came back from hunting before I came out of the woods, thinking that maybe Pa would go easier on me. I had been wrong—Pa just about wore me out with the same green switch for not doing my book learning and hiding from Ma.

Old Man Winter set in like he meant it, and the snow got deep quick. I felt safe and content. Hialeah was patiently trying to teach me how to sew one afternoon, when Cleo lifted her head and she suddenly became agitated. Cleo started growling in a low, menacing rumble and all of the hair on her back stood straight up. I jumped from my chair and reached for Pa's gun, but before I could reach it, the cabin door flew open, and Joe Walker fell to the floor. David, Hialeah and I ran for him at the same time. When I looked through the opening, I saw nothing but his horse and a trail of blood leading to the cabin door.

David was the first to speak. "He's been shot. Hialeah, boil up some water. Short Stack, fetch me anything we can make bandages out of. We're going to have get the bullet out."

I could hear what David was telling me, but I froze to the floor until he commanded me once more. "Short Stack, he's lost a lot of blood—get a move on."

David quickly lifted Joe from the floor and carried him to the closest bed, which happened to be mine. Hialeah boiled water from the snow outside, and I cut up cloth for bandages for the wound dressings as David had instructed. The twins had seen Joe Walker covered with blood, and I could see the fear in their eyes, but they didn't cry. I was proud of them both. Catlin and Clayton sat down in front of the fireplace and quietly watched, wide-eyed as a pair of owls.

I sat beside the bed, feeling helpless as David prepared to take the bullet out of Joe's shoulder.

"Short Stack, he's unconscious, but if he starts to move from a reflex of pain, you're going to have to hold him down."

I felt my stomach turn more than once as I watched David fade the knife into Joe's shoulder, searching for the bullet, but it was nothing compared to watching him fire a knife in the fireplace in order to sear the wound shut. The smell of the seared flesh was awful.

I knew Joe was in a bad way, but I still had to ask. "Is he going be all right?"

David's face looked grim. "He's lost a lot of blood, but he's young and strong. All we can do at this point is wait. I'm going out to tend to his horse and have a quick look around. Stay close to him if he wakes up. I'd be obliged to know what happened to him."

David left the cabin, tended to Joe's horse and was back within minutes, carrying someone else through the front door of the cabin. I could see panic in Hialeah's eyes when she whispered, "Waya." In the back of my mind, I recalled distantly that the word "Waya" meant "Wolf" in the Cherokee language. David laid him down on the closest available bed and gave us our orders once again.

"Boil up some more water and make up some more of those bandages. Waya took a bullet, too, but looks like the ice and snow slowed down the bleeding."

Hialeah was sitting solemnly by the fire, watching the flames dance in the fireplace. I had not heard her sweet melodic voice grace our cabin with song since the death of Austenaco. Hialeah was prayerfully singing one of the songs of her people, but it was a song I had never heard before. I wanted to go to her, but I could not leave David until Waya had been tended to. I watched him remove another bullet from another body and smelled the seared flesh once again.

Finally David whispered, "Well, I've done all I can do."

I bolted for the cabin door, thrust my head out into the freezing cold and retched until I finally regained control of my body, watching the steam slowly rising into the air from the frozen ground.

I walked back inside, and I rested one hand on the mantle of the fireplace. "Hialeah, how do you know Waya?"

She looked at me with tear-filled eyes. Hialeah pointed first to my brothers, and then to me. I understood what she was trying to tell me. Waya was her brother. I knelt down in front of her as she sat in Ma's rocker and wrapped my arms around her. I did not let go of her until the tears had been spent. I couldn't help but remember the moments of my life when I had needed someone to hold me, but cried alone. I know David felt bad for her too—I could see it in his eyes, and I heard it in his voice when he quietly spoke.

"We will have to take turns staying up tonight to keep watch over Joe and Waya. If either one of them show signs of fever then we need to keep them cooled off with wet clothes as best we can. I also want to make sure whatever trouble they stumbled onto doesn't come our way without us being prepared for it. I'll take the first watch."

CHAPTER 11
Dancing Butterflies

David woke me early the next morning for my watch. There was no need to wake Hialeah. Every hour I had spent sleeping, she had been sitting silently in Ma's rocker, gently rocking, watching over her brother. I could not help but wonder why Waya had never bothered to do the same for her. I understood the ways of the Cherokee wasn't like my way of doing things, but she had suffered so much alone without anyone in her family lifting a finger to help her, except Austenco. It just didn't make sense to me.

I added some logs to the fire and stoked it. I looked at her and felt a deep wash of compassion and love. It came to mind that I was becoming more and more like Ma every day, even if I did not want to be all ladylike in a dress. I was strong when I had to be, and I knew in my heart that strength would always be there for me to rely on. I was also smart enough to know that without the help of others, neither my brothers nor I would have survived. There had been Austenaco, Hialeah, David and Joe Walker.

I gently placed my hand on Hialeah's shoulder and softly whispered, "Hialeah, sleep. I will watch over him."

She had been reluctant to leave her brother, but finally she laid her body down. I sat in between Joe and Waya, and as I looked at Waya, something within me stirred. His face was so handsome, his chest firm and muscular, and his hair was black as night, long and silky. I pushed a lock of hair back from his forehead as he lay sleeping, and it was soft as cotton to the touch. It was then that I felt the fever beginning to burn beneath my touch. I picked up the water bucket, opened the cabin door, stepped outside and filled the wooden bucket plumb full of snow. I set the bucket right close to the fireplace and after the snow had melted, I kept cold, wet clothes swathed over Waya the rest of the night. He stirred some from the fever, but I managed to keep him still enough.

By late afternoon the following day, Joe was conscious and told us the story of their ordeal.

SHORT STACK

Walker heard tell the government had signed a peace treaty with the Cherokee. The government was supposed to provide the Cherokee with beef and supplies in exchange for more of their land. A constant stream of new settlers moving into the territory was destroying the Cherokee's territorial hunting grounds with each new cabin being built. The Cherokee were now starving, and the promised shipments had not arrived.

Once it became clear to Waya and Walker the meat and supplies were not coming, they set out to find the missing supplies. A band of Kiowa had attacked and killed the soldiers guarding the shipment and took the food meant for the Cherokee. Joe and Waya had ridden right into the middle of the skirmish, and both of them were fortunate to be alive.

It did not take Walker long to recover from his injury and return to his normal, obnoxious self. Waya had not regained consciousness, so either Hialeah or I were constantly tending to him. Even after all he'd been through and everything that had happened, Walker bantered the hours away pestering me. He could not resist the temptation to give my reins a sharp tug.

"You know, Short Stack, if'n I was Waya and could see you fawning all over me, holding my hand, and looking at me with them stars in your eyes, I reckon I would play sick for at least another week or more."

Most of the time, I ignored his comments and managed to keep myself busy, but David seemed to be right amused by his constant taunting. The first opportunity that presented itself, David flat out told me, "Short Stack, Walker is a mite sweet on you. Be careful!"

I really didn't pay much mind to what David was babbling about, as I figured he was just teasing me, too. I don't understand it to this very day—and like it even less—why menfolk get such a good belly laugh from teasing the womenfolk.

Four days later, Waya opened his eyes again for the first time since he'd been wounded. Hialeah immediately leapt to her feet and took his hand. I stood by and listened to them talk. I could only understand a word every now and then, so I really didn't feel like I was eavesdropping. After several moments, Hialeah turned to me with a beaming smile and introduced Waya to me.

When I asked her if he could understand my language, Joe quickly interrupted. "Waya speaks the language of the Cherokee, Short Stack. Is there something special you want me to tell him? After all, you have been looking awful moon-eyed over him for the last four days!"

Joe Walker had a stupid grin on his face that I

really didn't cotton to. I was beginning to feel flustered as I turned my back on Walker and looked at Waya, who was smiling with mischief at me.

"Hialeah, would you be kind enough to tell your brother I am pleased to meet him."

Before Hialeah could say a word, Waya took my hand and said, "Thank you most kindly for watching over me, Short Stack." I snatched my hand away from Waya, my face turning crimson, and I couldn't help but lose my temper as I turned on Walker.

"Joe, you lied to me! He understood every word we said."

His laughter exploded through the cabin. "I didn't exactly lie—I just didn't tell you the whole truth of it."

I felt so awkward and embarrassed, with no place to hide. I could feel the tears swelling up in my eyes. "If you will all excuse me, I have some chores that need tending to."

I grabbed my coat and left the cabin to feed the animals. Once I was out of sight of the cabin, I let the tears flow. Cleo had followed me out the door when I left the cabin—I guess she understood I needed a friend, or she maybe thought I might be going hunting. I walked to the shed, opened the door and sat down on the floor. Cleo laid down beside me and softly whined as I cried, snuggling her head into my lap. Within a couple of minutes, David opened the door. Hurriedly, I dried my tears with the back of my hand, but my eyes were red and swollen.

"Short Stack, you're exhausted. Why don't you try to get some sleep? Joe was just teasing. He didn't mean to hurt your feelings. If you ask me, I think Walker is a mite jealous of Waya." David flashed a warm smile, and then winked at me as he shut the door of the shed.

While David was trying to talk me into coming back to the cabin, my brothers were giving Joe Walker a pretty rough time of it. It was the first time my brothers had ever tried to take care of me or stand up for me. It took Joe quite by surprise when Catlin and Clayton both laid into him.

"You leave our sister alone!"

"You made her cry!"

"You're a big bully!"

When Walker laughed at my brothers, it was like throwing a lit match into kerosene. Catlin and Clayton attacked him at the same time, pulling his hair, biting and hitting him with everything they had. As David and I walked back inside the cabin, Hialeah was trying to pull the boys off of Joe, with Waya laughing heartily at the sudden turn of events.

I have to admit it: my brothers brought a smile

back to my face, and ended up I wasn't the one who forced the boys to behave, it was David. When the situation was finally brought under control, Hialeah and I quietly started to prepare supper, while David worked with the boys on their book learning in front of the fireplace.

Joe was sore, but well enough to sit at the table and move about some. Waya was still too weak to get up and around, so I prepared a plate for him. I tried to hand the prepared plate of food to Hialeah so she could serve her brother, but she smiled knowingly, politely declining as she sat down at her place at the table to eat. I really didn't think I was ready to face Waya, but I carried the plate to him. When I sat down beside him, a smile formed on his lips. I could feel the warmth of color on my face.

"If you help me with these pillows, I think I can sit up long enough to eat."

I helped him brace the pillows behind him and then handed him the plate of food. When I turned to leave the room, he spoke again.

"Short Stack, please don't worry about Joe. He just gets carried away sometimes. I truly appreciate everything you've done for me."

When I looked at him, there was kindness in his eyes and a gentleness to his smile. I still felt foolish, but I sat down in the chair beside his bed.

"How did you come to speak our language so well?"

Waya smiled as he began to eat. "I was sent east to study the customs of the white man and learn the language. My father thought it would improve our relationship with the white eyes. I can't see where my education has helped my people. What I have come to believe is that there is good and bad on both sides."

I guess I have always been bold, or maybe I just didn't think before I spoke. "Is that the reason you didn't come visit Hialeah?"

The smile from his face faded. "I didn't find out about my sister until I returned to my village," he replied gravely. "I must honor the ways of my people, Short Stack. But I will stay close to my sister and Adahy."

I took his plate when he finished and helped Hialeah do up the evening dishes. It had been a long day. I told everyone good night, and I made what I hoped was a graceful departure. I went to my room, put on my nightshirt and pulled back the covers from my bed. I had intended to lie down and go to sleep, but I kept thinking about the dress underneath my bed. I knelt down beside the bed and pulled out the box that was now covered with a fine layer of dust. I laid the box on my bed and opened it. Lying neatly folded inside the box was my dress of pink and burgundy. I sat down on the bed and carefully pulled the dress from the box. I held it in my arms for several moments before I stood up and took off my nightshirt. Carefully, I slipped the dress over my head, smoothing out the wrinkles with my hands. I stood looking in the mirror at my reflection and took the ribbon from my hair, letting my long auburn hair fall softly onto my shoulders. I picked up a hairbrush from the dresser and brushed my hair. When I looked at my reflection in the mirror, it made my heart flutter. I looked like Ma.

I had never intended for anyone to see me in the dress, but an unforeseen incident would turn my best intentions inside out. Cleo sounded the warning, barking wildly, and the animals outside started kicking up a fuss. I ran to fetch my gun from over the fireplace. David had been quicker than I—he was already headed out the front cabin door with his gun. I didn't even grab my coat, I just followed him. David was a couple yards ahead of me when I saw him take aim. I stopped and pulled Pa's gun to my shoulder just as the mountain lion squalled and leapt toward him—David had already fired the shot. He brought the mountain lion down in mid-air, and it tumbled to the ground. I lowered Pa's gun and walked up behind David to take a look at the dead animal. When David turned to face me, he suddenly forgot all about the mountain lion or calming down the animals in the stable.

"Lord have mercy, Short Stack! You freshen up to be one fine-looking young lady!"

I stared at David for a moment, and then I looked down at the dress I was wearing. I felt so confused and embarrassed I just ran back inside the cabin, but good ole Walker was standing there, just inside the cabin door.

"Why, you didn't have to get all dressed for me, Short Stack!"

I stared at him angrily, but I couldn't force back the tears from my eyes. Joe's laughter bellowed through the cabin, until a stern voice commanded him to stop. It was Waya.

"Joe, that's enough!"

I turned to see Waya trying to sit up. I glanced nervously from one to the other, as simmering looks were being exchanged. Finally, Waya looked my way and his expression portrayed only gentleness.

"Short Stack, please come sit with me awhile."

With pure devilment in my eyes, I stared down Joe Walker as I strolled over to Waya's bed and sat down next to him. When David walked back inside the cabin, Joe unloaded his anger with a booming voice.

"Since you're her Pa, I'm telling you straight

out: keep that Indian away from Short Stack. Ain't no good going to come of it, he will only bring her grief. Hell, she don't even know what a real man is!"

David stared down at Joe Walker, just like Pa would have done.

"Well Joe, I do believe she is a grown woman with a strong mind of her own. Short Stack can make up her own mind—she always does."

Walker quickly gathered his things together and lit out. After the dust had settled and Joe had made his departure, David turned and smiled at me. "I guess you got first watch tonight, Short Stack. Sweet dreams."

The cabin fell silent, and I was more than a little nervous. Waya thoughtfully gazed into my eyes—my body began to tremble. His hand touched the side of my face.

"You are beautiful—I don't blame Joe for being sweet on you."

I blushed underneath his gaze, not knowing what to do. He pulled me closer to him with the gentle touch of his hand. I felt his warm lips press against mine. I was no longer afraid or confused. I was a young woman in love with a basket full of butterflies dancing all around me.

CHAPTER 12
A Big Ole Rattler

I refused to think about the day Waya would be strong enough to return to his people. Lazy winter afternoons filled with conversation and laughter slipped by much too quickly in front of the fireplace with Hialeah, David, Waya and the boys. Waya had taken care to teach Hialeah a little more of my language during his stay with us. It made it a mite easier for her to understand the meaning of our words when she was able to translate them to and from her own language.

The day I had not wanted to see arrived like a thief in the night. I stood at the cabin door, waving goodbye with a forced smile on my lips, portraying an emotion I did not feel. I watched him ride away with tears in my eyes, but my place and my loyalty was with my brothers. Waya felt the same way about his people. I knew one day, Waya would return in passing, but it did not keep my heart from wanting him to stay.

The snow was beginning to slowly melt on the mountain, foretelling the arrival of spring. I cleaned my dress of pink and burgundy, placed it back in the box and stored it once again underneath my bed. With the arrival of spring, I would have no need of it.

David and I were out most every day, gathering our traps and making the necessary adjustments to the traplines. After talking it over with David, together we decided it was time to take Catlin and Clayton along with us when we ran the traplines. Both of my brothers seemed to grasp right off to running the traps, but they grumbled some about the preparations. They really didn't cotton to cleaning and greasing the traps, but if a body didn't keep the traps cleaned and greased, rust would eat away at them until they would become fragile and break.

I wanted to believe that when spring finally arrived and every daybreak promised a full day's work ahead of me, I would not have the time to think about Waya. But I have to admit sometimes my mind drifted a little. I became easily and often distracted—I really had to force myself to think about what I was doing. At night, it was another story. Once the sun set in the Tennessee sky, my heart and my mind would just take control. The glistening stars in the night sky above me would shine like diamonds, and they were just as bright as the stars in my eyes. I could dream for just a little while and recall with a breathless feeling a warm embrace, a gentle kiss, and two strong arms around me. I couldn't help but wonder if maybe Waya was gazing at the same stars that I was and thinking of me, too. I had never felt like this before, but it didn't feel strange to me. I was still getting my chores done and taking care of my brothers. I could dream a little, for I fully knew the truth of things: it just wasn't going to happen, but I found it was easy to block that reality from my daydreams.

After David and I had planted the garden and placed our traps along the river, I had a mind to build us a fence around the front of the cabin. David helped me split wood and stack it up till there was enough wood for us to start building the fence.

My brothers were getting a big kick out of running the trap lines with us. I had to keep a good eye on 'em, as they liked the water as much as I did, and I knew I had to let them play some. It was mostly fun at first for my brothers until the day David and I found a beaver inside one of the traps. My brothers turned a little green around the gills and looked away, making faces at each other. I wanted to laugh, but I somehow managed not to. I remembered the first time I saw Pa pull a beaver from the trap, it wasn't pretty, and when I watched Pa skin out the beaver hide, I turned more than just a little green—I lost my morning breakfast. My brothers didn't, and I felt a little swell of pride.

My brothers were already quickly learning the ways of the mountain, and I was proud of them. They tagged along after me everywhere I went, always asking questions about the trees or the animals. I answered their questions, trying to be patient just like Pa had done with me. Even though sometimes, I felt a little frustrated when their questions seemed endless. They would look at each other as if they were a mite confused when I answered a question, and then their innocent eyes would search mine. A few moments later, one of them would ask the same question for the third or fourth time.

The first part of early summer, David and I began to teach Catlin and Clayton how to shoot a rifle. They fared well, even though the rifle was mite heavy for them. Catlin seemed to take to shooting right off, but Clayton didn't cotton to the kick of the rifle or the sound it made when it fired. He would have to get used to it—learning to shoot a rifle was necessary for our way of life on the mountain. I felt Clayton was a lot like me. I had not cottoned to shooting a rifle right off, either. Ma had not wanted me to shoot a rifle any more than she liked me traipsing after Pa into the woods, but I did it anyway. I had to get used to the feel of it, the kick of it and I believed Clayton would too.

The first time Catlin and Clayton fired the rifle without me, they had no choice, they had done so together, side-by-side. David and I were hunting together in the woods just about two miles south of the cabin, when we heard the shot of the rifle and made fast tracks back to the cabin.

Hialeah had been working in the garden, keeping a watchful eye on little Adahy as he was played with my brothers in front of the cabin. A timber wolf had emerged from the woods, fast on the trail of a brown cottontail rabbit, but the rabbit led the wolf ran right up on the cabin, while the rabbit made fast tracks in the opposite direction. Cleo squared off her territory definitely, pacing back and forth in between her enemy and the boys. The wolf exposed long white teeth with a low vicious growl. Cleo faced the wolf with no fear—she was protecting the ones she loved. Everyone froze in their tracks, until the wolf charged and Cleo attacked.

It was more than obvious to my brothers: they didn't have much of a choice—they had to use the rifle to save the dog they loved or face losing her. They stood together holding the rifle, one behind the other. Clayton took careful aim and Catlin pulled the trigger. Both of them had been terrified, but together they had done one fine job, waiting for the right shot. When David and I reached the cabin, Cleo was lying within a couple yards of the wolf, whining softly. She was marked up some with a few scratches, but mostly seemed to just have the wind knocked out of her.

Our first concern was for Cleo. If the wolf had the sickness then it was likely that Cleo had been exposed to the deadly sickness during the fight. David quickly and gently tended to her, cleaning her wounds. Anyone in his or her right mind would have known from watching David care for Cleo just how much he loved her. But by nightfall of the very same day, he had built a large cage for Cleo. She would have to stay locked up in the cage until the next full moon. If she showed no signs of the sickness only then could we set her free. My brothers didn't cotton to locking up what they considered to be their dog, but we had no choice.

David and I found no visible signs of the wolf being sickly, but we could not take the chance—there was no real way of knowing just by looking at the wolf that now lay dead. We were a mite skittish about the body of the wolf, so to make sure no other animals came in contact with the wolf's body, David built a huge bonfire and burned it.

SHORT STACK

Even though the dog belonged to David, he didn't seem to mind the boys calling Cleo their dog. Catlin and Clayton gave David and me a rough time of it when Cleo softly whined to be freed from her cage, but we had to stand firm and keep her confined.

When the next full moon adorned the Tennessee sky, and the critical time had finally passed, Cleo showed no signs of the illness. I decided to mark Cleo's day of freedom with a special meal of celebration. Hialeah and I searched the woods until we found some wild elderberries to make pies. I helped her wash and drain the berries, and then Hialeah baked the pies. I really wanted some blackberry pies, but the blackberries had not come on yet. David picked sweet ear corn from our garden and some sweet red tomatoes. Hialeah cooked venison over the fire and baked up some mouth-watering fresh bread.

That night Cleo was given a feast of venison and fresh bread. I was happy and relieved to see Cleo jumping all over my brothers and playing with them. We ate, laughed and watched the fire burn low into the night. When it was time for bed, my brothers started a ruckus over who Cleo was going to sleep with, so they slept in the same bed with Cleo between them. Early the next morning, David, my brothers and I set out to check on our traps along the river.

It was just about mid morning when Joe Walker rode up on us with a friendly greeting. "Morning, Short Stack."

I turned away, refusing to respond.

David finally broke the silence. "Morning Joe, what brings you up this way?"

Joe climbed down from his horse, striding a little closer to David. "I was trailing a deer on the south ridge of the mountain, when I saw you from the crest of the ridge. I just wanted to ride down to say thanks. You saved my life. I ain't likely to forget that."

With that said Joe tipped his hat politely and walked back over to his horse. He hesitated for a moment with his hands on the saddle of his horse. He wouldn't—or couldn't—face me.

"I'm sorry, Short Stack."

Joe Walker hauled himself back into the saddle, and he did not look back as rode away into the midday sun. I stood there for a moment, not really knowing what to think about Joe Walker's unexpected apology.

As I turned back toward the cabin, I suddenly caught a glimpse of movement in the high grass next to Catlin and Clayton. I screamed at my brothers with terror in my eyes. Timber rattlesnakes are well-known in these parts, especially in the

SHORT STACK

woods. The dark rings of brown against lighter rings of gray make it difficult to spot a rattler in the woods, but in the green grass, it was plain as warts on a toad frog.

"Boys, stop! Stop! Clayton! Catlin! Don't move!" I hissed through clenched teeth.

David and I slowly walked toward my brothers. We froze and stared at each other when we heard the snake's ominous rattle. When the timber rattler feels threatened, it shakes the coil of its tail. Hollow buttons are added onto its tail every time the rattler sheds its skin, creating the rattling sound so feared in these parts. Once the warning has been given, the snake is ready to strike. I moved closer to Catlin, seeing movement about a yard from him.

"I see it, David!" I whispered harshly. "Catlin! Stand still!"

I really can't blame Catlin for not listening to me. He was terrified and overwhelmed with panic. Meantime, Catlin bolted for the cabin. I didn't have time to aim my rifle or even think about what I was doing, I just did it. I jumped for Catlin, grabbing him away from the rattler, hoping David could fire his rifle fast enough to kill the snake before it had the chance to strike. It might have worked, except the rattler was already in mid-strike when I jumped for Catlin. The rattler caught the side of my right leg. Before the snake could strike again, David fired his rifle.

Walker had not been very far away when he heard the rifle fire and rode back. My leg hurt something awful—it burned like fire. Catlin kept telling me he was sorry, over and over again. I tried my best to calm him down and reassure him that I would be all right.

"Now don't you worry none, Catlin. I'm going to be just fine."

David was cutting through my britches, tending to the snakebite when Walker rode back up and quickly dismounted his horse. "What happened to her David?"

David was trying to hurry, cutting away my britches leg to get to the bite wound. He didn't even turn around to look at Joe when he spoke. "A big ole rattler decided to tangle with Short Stack."

Walker ran to me and dropped to his knees beside David. "You ever cut a snake bite before? If you ain't, move over, I'll do it."

David quickly moved out of the way and Joe took the knife from his hand. I was already feeling a mite sick and light-headed when Joe picked up a small fallen branch from an oak tree and put it between my teeth like a riding bit, telling me to bite down. Then he cut my skin in two places on either side of the bite and tried to withdraw the poison from my leg. After tending to my wound, Joe

SHORT STACK

hurried over to his horse, pulled down a blanket and wrapped it tightly around me.

"David, after I mount up, hand Short Stack up here to me. I've got to take her to the Cherokee camp. They can help her. Don't let it furrow your brow none. I've seen the Cherokee treat many a snake bite."

David quickly picked me up and then delivered me into Walker's waiting arms. The fever of the snakebite was already burning through my body when I fell asleep in Joe's arms. I don't remember much about the rough, bumpy journey to the Cherokee camp, but I do remember the young Indian brave who pulled me down from Joe's horse. I looked into his eyes and whispered, "Waya."

CHAPTER 13
Betrayed

I don't recall much of anything for the next few days except the steady lyrical chant of music that seemed to drift clean through me like a satin cloud, soothing and peaceful. I remember the young Cherokee braves, dancing by the firelight to the slow rhythm of the drums, casting their mystic shadows onto the walls of the teepee.

I awoke from the haze of sleep two days later in the early morning hours, before the sun crested the mountain ridge. I was still feeling weak, but I gave it thunder and managed to sit up. My leg ached and was still swollen, but I also knew the immediate danger had passed. Slowly I shook my head, recalling the events that had brought me to the Cherokee encampment. I looked into the smoldering coals of the campfire and pulled the blanket a little tighter about me.

The next thought to cross my mind was of my brothers, especially Catlin. They must be worried something awful about me. I had to get home. My clothes were neatly folded beside me, and I was right grateful someone had taken the time to clean my clothes. But it also came to mind that someone had to have taken them off me, and that thought made me feel a mite uneasy. I prayed it hadn't been Walker who had stripped me down.

Looking across the teepee, I saw a young Indian girl sleeping on a pallet on the far side of the fire. She was so beautiful—her long, silky hair was as black as the raven. After several moments, I stoked the fire and added a few more pieces of wood to the rekindled blaze. The young Indian girl slowly opened her eyes and looked at me. Sitting up, she smiled innocently at me, and then tried patiently to find out if I was hungry using simple hand gestures. When I eagerly nodded my head, the girl left the teepee and quickly returned with a bowl of venison.

I had just about finished eating when the flap of the teepee opened. I wasn't surprised to see Waya, but I was a little flustered to see Joe Walker walk in right behind him. I looked at them both. Joe Walker was standing there with a smile on his face, and Waya was looking at me with worried eyes.

"I'm right grateful to both of you for helping me the way you did. I know I was in a bad way, and

SHORT STACK

I'm much obliged for your help. Waya, I need to borrow a horse. I have to get back to my brothers. They must be worried something awful about me."

Waya spoke softly, his deep voice tempered with kindness and concern. "You should rest at least another day before you try to make the long journey home."

Joe Walker quickly volunteered, "Short Stack, if you're a mind to get yourself home, I'll take you straight away."

I didn't know what to make of the situation. Once again, tensions between Waya and Joe Walker seemed to be raging somewhere along the borderline of fire and brimstone. I looked at Waya and then Joe Walker as they exchanged angry looks. A knife could have cut clean through the tension in the air, but instead, it was the young Indian girl, now standing by Waya, who broke the silence. I could not understand her words, but Joe abruptly smiled and then nearly choked with amusement.

"Waya, where are your manners? Don't you think you should introduce Short Stack to the young lady?"

Several moments went by before Waya faced me. He looked me right in the eye and then broke my heart. "Short Stack, this is Ayita. She belongs to me."

Sharon A. Cantor

My mind was racing, and then for some reason I suddenly recalled the translation of the young squaw's name: "Ayita: First to Dance."

I was still groggy and a mite confused, so I quickly interrupted him. "Are you trying to tell me this woman is your *wife*?"

While Joe Walker was actually looking downright proud of himself, Waya did not falter as he continued, "I am the son of a chief. I must also sire a son, Short Stack, a Cherokee son. I did not mean for you to be hurt."

With that said, Waya turned and left the teepee. I wanted to cry, but I didn't. I was too stubborn and proud to give Walker the satisfaction of my tears.

Angrily I glared at Joe. "I'll be ready to light out of here before you can saddle the horses. Now get out!"

Joe pulled the flap of the teepee open and then stopped abruptly to face me with no emotion showing on his face. "Short Stack, you were warned. You do not understand the ways of the Cherokee. A Cherokee brave can have many squaws."

Joe faltered for a moment and then continued, "The choice is up to you. I'll saddle the horses."

After Walker left the teepee, I sat alone by the fire. My body trembled with the swirling passions of heartache and wounded pride. Waya had made me feel like a woman for the first time in my life. Becoming a woman was a special feeling, but love itself had left me facing nothing but a passel of frustration and hurt.

Slowly, I began putting my clothes back on. I now had more than one reason to light out for home. My leg was still a little sore and I knew it would slow me down some, but I couldn't wait to leave. I never wanted to see Waya again. I knew I couldn't bring myself to hate him, but I didn't think I could bring myself to ever look into his eyes again either. The truth had been in front of me the whole time, but I had chosen to ignore it.

By the time I had climbed into my clothes and walked outside, Walker was waiting patiently with the horses. Waya was holding the reins of my horse. I stopped and glanced at him just long enough to show him eyes as cold as a frozen creek in the dead of winter. Out of pure spite, I let Walker assist me when I could not pull myself into the saddle of my horse.

My leg was still too swollen to support the weight of my own body long enough for me to mount the horse. The pain was nearly unbearable. Without hesitation, I let Joe pick me up with his big hands that ever so gently encircled my waist. When I looked into his eyes, they sparkled with humor, but he was not mocking me—in fact, I saw sympathy, and maybe even a little compassion for my situation. When we rode out of the Cherokee encampment, I never looked back. Walker had not seen the tears in my eyes and neither would Waya.

Walker and I rode in silence through the woods toward home. The trees were covered with pink blossoms. It was so beautiful, but the peaceful feeling the woods always gave me was just not there. I wanted to cry, I wanted to scream, yet I was stubborn enough to hold back the pain. Pa would have done the same thing.

I expected to see my brothers run out of the cabin from a country mile away, but when we were within sight of the cabin, all was still and quiet. Joe held up his hand to alert me to stop and I did. Before he said a word, I knew he was right. A grim warning echoed through the woods, without making a sound.

"Short Stack, hold up a spell. Something just doesn't feel right to me."

I turned my horse around and went back into the cover of the trees. I climbed down off my horse, bracing the weight of my body against my one good leg, and then I pulled Pa's gun down from the saddle. This was the very spot where I had stayed hidden the day my family had been killed. It felt like I was walking over my own grave. Joe signaled for me to wait, and then he started for the cabin. If I had stayed put, he would have died that day.

I waited until he was within six or seven yards of the cabin before I followed him. I searched the edge of the trees surrounding the cabin. From the right side of the cabin, I caught a reflection of light. I felt right certain the dancing sparkle of sunshine was bouncing off the barrel of a rifle. I knew I could shoot that far, but I didn't want to shoot unless I knew exactly who I was shooting at. I circled back and crept up behind the cabin. There was a gnawing edge of fear and guilt in my heart for my brothers as I waited for something to happen.

Several minutes slipped by before I got close enough to see the young Kiowa warrior who now had his rifle aimed at Joe's back. I braced myself against the side of a maple tree and took careful aim. I had no choice—I pulled the trigger. Joe spun around to face me with a startled look on his face, and then jumped for cover behind the woodpile. I stood beside that tree waiting for all hell to break loose, but all was as quiet as a church full of sinners.

Joe took his time searching the woods, and once again started for the cabin. I couldn't stand it any longer—I wanted to see my brothers. I had to find out what had happened. I was almost to the cabin door when Walker restrained me with a right smart amount of force.

"Short Stack, do yourself a favor and don't go in there."

Refusing to listen to him, I jerked free, half-stumbling through the front door of the cabin. I took three or four more unsteady steps as my eyes desperately searched the cabin. I couldn't believe everything I had worked endless hours for had been destroyed. I saw Hialeah lying on the floor next to the fireplace, and my heart ached with the love I felt for her. I should have gone to her, but instead, I just stood there, afraid to look for the others, the heart-stopping fear of not knowing what I might find rooting me to the floor. Panic finally just took over, and I ran through the cabin screaming at the top of my lungs for my brothers.

"Catlin! Clayton! It's Short Stack. I'm home! Where are you? Catlin! Clayton!"

My screams echoed through the empty cabin. I felt a sob escape my lips, I felt the tremors of my body as I slowly knelt beside Hialeah, gently gathering her up in my arms, her body already beginning to cool. The cold hands of death now held her too. I pulled a blanket from the bed and tenderly wrapped it around her.

Walker was searching the area around the cabin to make sure there were no other Kiowa braves scouting around. When he walked back into the cabin, I was sitting in front of the fireplace, still smoldering with dying coals.

"Short Stack, I'm sorry. I've heard rumors about the Indian tribes joining together to fight for their land, but it never dawned on me that something like this might happen. You're not safe here."

I was angry, frustrated and emotionally spent.

"Walker, damn you! Where the hell are David, Catlin, Clayton and Adahy? I won't go! I won't go without my brothers! I won't go without my family!"

Joe's faced turned solemn. "Short Stack, I hope for your sake that when the Indians found Catlin and Clayton, they did not take a notion to hurt them. You have to believe there is a good chance your brothers are still alive. The Kiowa believe they possess great magic because they are identical twins. As for David, let's just hope he wasn't here when the Kiowa attacked. David might be tracking your brothers right now."

Suddenly, I thought of little Adahy. "Joe, what about Adahy? He's a half-breed. What will they do to him?"

Joe looked away and did not answer my question. I was shaking all over with fear and anger. I picked up the closest thing to me and started throwing a first class fit. Joe let me carry on a spell before he tried to calm me down. I refused to listen to him or let him control me. My whole life had been turned upside down again. I know Pa wouldn't have carried on in such a way, but I didn't care! I didn't stop screaming until I thought I heard a faint whimper. I froze in my tracks and tried with all my might to hear it again.

"Walker, did you hear that? Walker, please help me!" Both of us tiptoed cautiously, searching around the cabin. I had taken four or five steps when I heard the whimpering sound again.

"Joe, its Adahy! Adahy, where are you, baby? It's Short Stack! I'm home, it's all right."

The next sound I heard came from beneath my feet, the floor of the cabin and Pa's secret hiding place for ammunition. Hialeah had died over the trap door, sacrificing herself to keep her son hidden from the Kiowa. Plumb took over with emotion, I pulled Hialeah to one side as Walker yanked the boards from the floor with everything he had. Huddled beneath the floor, afraid and crying in a place not any bigger than a crawlspace, we found Adahy. His little face was streaked with tears, his little hands reaching for me with fear in his eyes. I picked up Adahy and kept him cradled against me until Joe had taken Hialeah from the cabin. Hialeah was no kin to me, even though I felt like she was. I loved Adahy—he carried Pa's name and that was

SHORT STACK

good enough for me. I would do right by Hialeah, what she would want me to do. Adahy was now my son.

Walker stubbornly tried to convince me to leave the mountain with Adahy. "Short Stack, the Indian tribes have joined together to fight the white man and more tribes will join them. The Kiowa, the Creek and the Seminole have already joined forces with the Cherokee. Believe me, Short Stack, they mean business! The white-eyes have lied to them too many times, and now the Indians are on the warpath, and they are hell-bent on staying on their land. You and Adahy are not safe here."

I did not hesitate. "Walker, my brothers may still be alive, and I intend to stay put until my brothers come home! If I leave here, they won't know where to find me."

Later that night, David returned to the cabin, and we were surely relieved to see him walk through the cabin door. The Kiowa had attacked the cabin while he was out running the traps. He heard the rifle fire and came running, but by the time he reached the cabin, the fighting was over and Hialeah was dead. David set out to track the Kiowa Indians. He had not known Adahy was hidden in the cabin. He eventually lost their trail and returned to the cabin. I know it was hard for him to face me without my brothers. I was angry and determined to go after my brothers, but neither David nor Walker would listen to me.

Joe stayed on a spell to help us put the cabin back together and to make sure I didn't try going off after my brothers alone. The day he rode out, he gave me one final warning.

"If you're a mind to raise Adahy, cut his hair and make him look like he is your son, or the whites will kill him before the Indians do."

Stretching in the saddle and looking toward the east, Joe continued, "David, keep running your traps, but keep a good eye out and watch for signs. I'll be back with supplies long before winter has a chance to set in."

I handed Joe some dried venison and I looked him right in the eye. "Walker, please look for my brothers."

He looked at me with a mixture of anger and concern in his eyes. "Don't do anything stupid, Short Stack. If your brothers are alive, any foolishness will likely get them killed. I'm going to do some tracking of my own. If I find or hear tell of them, I'll send word. You stay safe now, you hear?"

CHAPTER 14
The Loss of Adahy

I kept doing whatever needed to be done, it was just like the way of things. Didn't matter how much I grieved, the sun would still rise and set. But not a solitary day went by that my brothers didn't come to mind. Where were Clayton and Catlin? Did they have enough to eat? Did they have warm clothing? The question that ate away at me the most, day after day, and gave me pause each time it came to mind: were my brothers waiting for me to find them? I grieved for them something fierce, but I never gave up hope that someday I would see Catlin and Clayton again. I celebrated my brothers' passing birthdays each and every year, with either a pie or a cake, depending on what supplies I had on hand.

I watched Adahy grow into a fine-looking young man, and he loved the mountain as much as I did. He knew every inch of it—the trees, the hills and valleys, the beautiful and the deadly. What I hadn't taught him about the mountain, Waya had. Adahy even learned to read animal signs better than I. He could read the tracks of any animal on the mountain and trail a deer for a country mile, even after the trail had grown cold.

On those rare and awkward occasions, it pained me some to see Waya, but I needed his friendship and protection now more than ever. I had come to understand that I had been foolhardy, with a mind full of girlhood dreams, and I was just too young to know any better. Some lessons in life have to be learned the hard way. Waya would leave fresh meat outside the cabin door every now and again to help us. The meat would already be dressed up just fine, ready to cook. Waya had also taken on the responsibility of making sure Adahy knew the ways and language of the Cherokee.

I saw Walker from time to time, when he stopped by to check up on us. The grim look on his face always told the same story: there had been no word on the whereabouts of my brothers. I know he hated to face me with no news to chew on concerning my brothers.

I had also come to know that young Lieutenant Michael Walker was Joe Walker's brother. Joe had spoken to him, requesting that he keep a lookout for my brothers. The banter between them had not been focused on David—or my 'Pa' as he was known. We would have been in a world of hurt if their conversation had turned toward David. I confided as much to David, letting him know whenever Walker was around, I would have to call him 'Pa.' Walker, if nothing else had been a good friend, whether I had wanted one or not, and he had saved my hide more than once. But I could not yet bring myself to trust him with my dark secrets and lies—or David's life.

All the while, as each day passed, there was a constant fret due to the ongoing skirmishes between the Indians and the new settlers coming into the territory. Settlers obtained land either by lottery or from land parceled out and sold off by the *government*. It didn't seem to matter that the land wasn't theirs to begin with. More soldiers were being dispatched to the territory to protect the growing number of white settlers against Indian attacks. I just didn't see the need for all the bloodshed, especially since there were innocent women and children dying on both sides.

From time to time, I would hear rumors and stories of Clayton and Catlin, but nothing I could really take stock in. Joe would always tell me anything he heard tell of concerning my brothers. Some folks passing through would say my brothers were seen living with the Kiowa Indians. Some folks came right out with it and said my brothers were dead. While others heard tell they had run off to hunt buffalo in the plains after escaping from the Kiowa. For me, it was as plain as the nose on my face: somewhere, my brothers were still alive.

The settlement around the trading post had quickly grown, adding a blacksmith shop, a stable, a saloon and a general store where a body could buy most anything. I didn't go into town unless there was a need to. I wasn't much good at socializing with the town folks. After all, they were all good Christian folks with families, and I was the mother of an illegitimate half-breed son. It didn't make me no nevermind.

On one of my chance visits to the general store, I met a young girl named Molly, and I liked her right off. She wasn't like most folks in town who set their nose in the air if'n they crossed my path. I found out from Walker that Molly worked at the saloon in town, and Molly wasn't her given name.

Molly had come to be ashamed of her lot in life. She had traveled to Tennessee by wagon train with her husband as a new bride. They would settle the land they had purchased and begin their lives together raising crops and children. Unfortunately, the wagon train had been attacked by Indians and her husband had been killed. It did not matter that Molly held the deed to the land marked 'paid in full' in her hands. The claims office would not allow her to take ownership of the land without a husband. Her land was sold at auction to the highest bidder for a mere pittance of the price she and her late husband had paid for it.

Each time I made a visit to the general store, I made sure that I dropped by to visit Molly at the saloon. I know our friendship turned some heads and set some tongues to wagging in town, but to me, that was neither here nor there. I reckon they just didn't have anything better to chew the fat on.

David's life had been buried in the past, long forgotten over the years. He was well-known to the folks in the settlement, but he was known there by the name of Jethro. David had asked me more than once to move into the settlement where it would be safer for Adahy and me, but each time I refused. David finally gave up asking and moved to the settlement himself, eventually getting hitched to the young school teacher he had been courting. I can't say I blame him none for living his own life. His wife was a beautiful and proper young lady named Katherine Murphy.

Katherine had taught school back in Illinois. I heard tell the folks around the settlement were building a school house for her to teach the growing number of children in town. Her family had won some sort of government lottery for a parcel of land that the government had purchased from the Cherokee.

I wasn't well thought of around the settlement for more than one reason. I had tangled with some of the new settlers when they tried settling on my land. I wasn't about to let folks start cutting down the trees on my mountain. Some of them offered me money for the land, but I refused. This mountain cradled my family in its bosom, and I would never let go of it. If not for David, the claims office might have taken my home, my land, and sold it to settlers. David had done right by me in that respect.

The local gossip around the settlement was that I had a child out of wedlock, an illegitimate half-breed son of a Cherokee brave. In other words, I was a woman of ill repute with an even worse disposition when riled. I couldn't argue none about my fiery disposition, for just looking at some of those prissy women made me want to slap some good ole common sense into them, but I just went about my business and paid no mind to their wagging tongues. I loved Adahy, and I took no stock in their gossip. The women who gossiped about me had husbands who visited Molly at the saloon without fail at least every other week.

I was happy to see Waya ride up to the cabin one afternoon, but he rode up with three other

SHORT STACK

braves, and that gave me pause. Usually, he would ride up alone. Waya explained to me that the Cherokee tribe was being forced to move onto a reservation soon. It was just a matter of time.

The Kiowa, Cheyenne, Apache, Comanche and other tribes had tried to fight the white man, but it was proving to be a losing proposition. The Cherokee, along with other tribes, was being moved nigh onto eight hundred miles from Tennessee to the Oklahoma Territory. Waya had wanted to take Adahy with him. I refused without even thinking about it. I knew that over the years, the Cherokee had become more like what the townsfolk were calling 'civilized.' Even though the Cherokee had become farmers, adapting to the ways of the white man more than most other tribes, I was afraid Adahy would still be an outsider amongst the Cherokee. I knew Waya truly believed in his heart that Adahy would be better off with the Cherokee and, looking back on it, I should have listened.

The year was 1838, and I had not laid eyes on my brothers for ten long years. I was going on twenty-five years old. Waya had honored my wishes and did not take Adahy from me, and I was thankful. I don't think I could have lived through the pain of one more loss. Adahy was all I had left.

The blue coat soldiers came two days later, and

despite the kicking and screaming fit I pitched, they took Adahy from me with me cussing and spitting at them. They called me an Indian lover and a whore. I was not used to being so outnumbered or feeling so helpless. I didn't cotton to these feelings at all. I cried for two days and prayed for Walker or Waya to return and help me, but I was on my own.

When I felt I could not wait any longer, I set my mind to follow the soldiers myself and find Adahy. The cabin, the mountain, and my family had meant everything to me, and now it was all gone. Everything I had worked for. I would not sit back and let a bunch of idiots take my son without a fight. I had a young mare who was full of fight and spirit, and I knew that I would need a strapping horse to make this journey. Most white folks did not give a damn about the Indians, and most Indians didn't give a lick for the white eyes, either. I could understand both sides of this conflict, but the young boy I now claimed as my son was an innocent victim in all this. I made up my mind that I would not return to this mountain without Adahy.

Even if it killed me.

For the first time in my life, I was truly alone. The anger that burned inside me was unquenchable. I just did not give a lick for the gossip about me among my own people. My own kind had accused the Indians of being cruel and unjust, but I saw my

SHORT STACK

own kind doing the same sort of bad things and worse.

The day I rode into the trading post, the men sitting outside the store eyed me with disgust. I still had Pa's rifle after all those years, and I had two pistols hanging from my gun belt. I knew—and so did they—that I would not hesitate to use them. I had nothing to lose.

I was thankful to Joe Walker for giving me the pistols and the gun belt. The pistols wasn't much good for distance like my rifle was, but up close they did a right fine job. I walked into the trading post and ordered coffee, bacon, gunpowder and lead for my rifle and pistols. The bald-headed man behind the counter stared at me with hate burning in his eyes.

"I don't sell supplies to folks who are friendly with the Indians. As a matter of fact, I won't sell supplies to a whore who consorts with Injuns."

I looked at him with pure disgust. "Mister, I have lived on this mountain all my life. My money is just as good as any church-going folk in this settlement. I don't like to put up a fuss, but I can shoot this here rifle just as straight as any man. Fill my order before I become uneasy."

I could tell right off he did not take me seriously. His eyes mocked me, and I just couldn't stand any more grief. I fired a shot from my pistol into the floor about an inch from the shopkeeper's right foot. A small crowd of people began to gather outside of the front door just to see the commotion.

"Mister, my patience is running a mite thin these days. Just fill my order, and I will be on my way."

Several men had gathered outside, but none of them dared to step through the doorway of the general store. I got my supplies without another word spoken from the nervous shopkeeper. I walked through the staring crowd that had gathered and loaded up my horse. I rode out of the settlement determined more than ever to find Adahy. I would find the young boy I loved, and we would go back to the mountain together, or I wouldn't come back at all. I would kill anyone who decided to get in my way.

I followed the trail left by the soldiers, which even a blind fool could have followed. There were a good number of horses and at least two wagons, likely loaded down with supplies for the soldiers. They were at least a two day's ride ahead of me, but the wagons would slow them down considerable. I hated leaving the cabin. It would be easy pickin's for squatters, but the way I looked at it, without a family tending to it, that old cabin just didn't feel like a home, anyway.

CHAPTER 15
Trail of Tears

I didn't want to wait for daylight. I had already dawdled too long. I knew the mountain even in the dark, and I could travel until my surroundings became unfamiliar. I had a full harvest moon shining down on me—I would just have to take it slow.

Cleo had passed on a few years back, but she had a litter of five pups and all were of good stock. I gave four of the pups to other folks, and I kept one of them. Right off, I knew he had a good sense about him—he was playful, and yet quick to notice any sound of a possible threat.

I didn't name him straight away. I wanted to give him a name that would suit him right down to the ground. He was as fast as a bullet when it came to chasing rabbits and other wild game, and so, he earned the name of Bullet. He was the best tracker in these parts, and he was a fierce protector. There was a lot of wolf in him, but he was gentle and always obeyed my call. That dog loved to hunt so much. I had never seen the like in a dog before, but since I'd only owned two of them, I couldn't rightly tell for sure. He looked a lot like his mother with long, straight hair with colors of silver and black silhouetted against a deep golden brown around his face, but he had the heart of the wolf. I had a favorite hunting spot in the woods. I would sit down on this fallen tree just north of the cabin and wait. Bullet would take off, running the rabbits right to me, along with an occasional deer. I knew if anyone could track Adahy, it would be Bullet.

 I had brought with me a piece of clothing Adahy had worn before the soldiers had taken him, and I knew the garment still held his scent. I didn't have to pack much: ammunition, biscuits, a canteen, a bed roll and some beef jerky. Ready or not, my journey began as I held out the shirt to Bullet. He sniffed the garment all over and started wagging his tail so hard I thought he was fixing to fly.

 At first, it was right easy trailing the soldiers, as they left plenty of sign to follow. The moon was so full and bright it made the shadows dance, making the traveling a damn sight better than I feared it was going to be. I found a place to camp about six hours later, but I did not make a campfire. I scouted

SHORT STACK

the area thoroughly before settling down to sleep. Bullet laid down beside me, and we shared a few biscuits and some beef jerky. I got along a whole lot better with Bullet than I did most folks.

I sat there in the darkness petting Bullet, just mulling things over in my head. I really didn't have a plan. First I had to find Adahy, and then I had to get past the soldiers. I had reacted with such fury and hate, it seemed I had gone and lost all of my good sense, but I didn't care. If this turned out badly, I just hoped someone would take a mind to lay my bones in the ground alongside my family.

Walker had been right about the tribes banding together, but in the end, they still lost their freedom and their land. There were five Indian Nations, which came to be called the "Civilized Tribes:" the Choctaw, the Creek, the Chicasaw, the Seminole and the Cherokee. I heard tell they were moving the Cherokee to some godforsaken place over eight hundred miles away. They called this place a reservation, but it sounded to me like a fancy word for hell on earth. The Cherokee were being forced to leave the land of their fathers, sacred ground, and none of the Indian tribes would ever see their homes again. It just wasn't right, no matter what direction I looked at it from. It just wasn't right.

Several years earlier, that high society fellow up in affairs of state and country by the name of

Sharon A. Cantor

Andrew Jackson organized like-minded folk, and they passed laws to take the land from the Indians. Once the storied general who'd defeated the Red Stick Creeks so soundly in 1814, he'd wound up as President of these here United States. Among other names, the Indians called him *Sharp Knife*. Seemed to me folks had traded crown, royalty and riches from the old country for nigh on to the same ole thing, just named up different.

Gold had been discovered right smack dab in the middle of the Cherokee country, which only fueled the fires of *Greed*. Folks like Jackson hadn't lived up on the mountain, and they sure as hell didn't know the Cherokee. They were simple farmers, just trying to protect their land and families.

It didn't make me no nevermind what color your skin was, if'n you did right by me, I did right by you. Those city folks just didn't live like I did. Let them come down to my neck of the woods and live a spell then maybe they might understand this way of life. Or then again, maybe they wouldn't.

I couldn't see city folks lasting one single day out here: chopping wood, fetching water from the creek, hunting in the woods, waiting without complaint for that perfect shot to bring home supper, even if it took hours. setting traps down along the river, knee deep in mud. Running them traps near daily, and if you were lucky enough to pull a beaver from one, it'd be skinning time.

Depending on the weather, if'n it was a warm windy day then a body had to make time to wash clothes in the creek on the washboard and then hang the clothes on the line to dry. On rainy days, you would set your mind to making the soap needed to wash the clothes, that being a concoction of boiled pig fat and water hand-carried from the river, poured through the ashes of a wood fire. I didn't do so well with making soap, but it was good enough to keep us clean.

On a daily basis, cooking consisted of basic meat simmering over the fireplace for most of the day. Vegetables in summer were mostly fresh from the vine, but in winter you had to use fruits, vegetables and herbs you had dried during the summer. Nope, I seriously doubt them city folks would cotton to our way of life.

I stirred from my sleep when Bullet began to softly growl in a low tone of warning. At the same time, he lifted my left arm with his snout. When I opened my eyes, I'd have sworn David and Walker were both sitting close enough to me that I could have spit on them. Without even thinking about what I was doing, I was reaching for my rifle before it dawned on me who I was staring at.

David was the first to start flapping his jaws,

scolding me like I was still a kid. "What the hell did you think you were doing running off like that? I got a mind to take you across my knee!"

Walker damn near choked on his own laughter as he said, "Now, I would pay good money to see that!"

I stood to my feet, solemnly gazing at both of them. "Both of you can wipe them God all mighty, puckered up scowls off your faces. Hell, you both remind me of the north end of a southbound mule. I have lost too many folks I love, and I am feeling a mite raw. It don't matter to me anymore how this turns out. This is who I am, and this is what I have my mind set to do. Adahy was alive the last time I saw him. I have lost pert' near my whole family, but I know where the last one is headed, and come hellfire and brimstone, I'm going to bring him home, or die trying."

My defiant eyes were burning with fire, but I could feel the tears beginning to spring up, and it only made me feel more enraged with myself. I threw my hands into the air, raised my voice and screamed at David, "The Cherokee are calling this the passage to the reservation: *Nunna Dual Isunyi*—the Trail Where They Cried. Come hell or high water, I will find Adahy. So now, which one of you wants to tell me how y'all figured out what I was up too?"

SHORT STACK

Walker half-heartedly smiled, but spoke up firmly. "You kicked up quite a fuss at the trading post. Folks have all been chewing the fat considerable over your visit. Your Pa—uh—David and I were pretty much in accord you'd see fit to go off half-cocked, so we brought along some friends. But I do declare, woman, you are as stubborn as a Missouri mule, and you're likely going to be the death of me afore it's all said and done."

From the shadow of the trees, Waya stepped into the circle of firelight between Walker and me. The moonlight fell on his skin like a whisper, but for the first time in my eyes, he was just a man. Waya called out in the voice of the night owl, and six young warriors walked into the circle, forming up behind him. I was stunned into silence. I had gone to sleep with only a loyal dog beside me, feeling alone, just like I felt when Pa died.

Looking into Waya's eyes, I said slowly, "The soldiers, they took Adahy. I couldn't stop them. I should have listened to you."

Waya stepped closer to me and knowingly looked into my eyes. "I know. Your love for Adahy runs deep and strong, like the river. Let me help you get him back."

Sudden realization dawned on me, and I grabbed a firm hold of Waya's arm. "Wait just a damn minute! I heard tell the soldiers raided your village! How did you get away from the soldiers?"

"Short Stack, our warriors were hunting when the soldiers raided our village. We were promised food that never arrived. Our people were starving. When our warriors returned with meat to feed our people, there was nothing left but the blackened earth. The soldiers had taken our women, the children and the elderly. There was no one left, and the village had been burned. I am looking for my wife and son. I will go on with you or without you."

I eyed him with anger, flashing fire from my eyes. "I don't reckon I have the patience of Job! Don't you be getting all uppity on me Waya! I know your kinfolk are just as downright important as mine. I understand you love your son, and he might be the son of a chief, but Adahy is just as important to me as your son is to you."

I picked up my blanket and then rolled it up into my saddlebag. Mounting my horse I told the men around me: "Better get a move on. They still have a jump on us. You all try and keep up. Bullet, come."

We rode in silence for hours, and it came to mind that Walker had at first had called David 'Pa' and then stammered some, changing it to 'David.' I slowed up the pace of my horse, so I was riding alongside David. I kept my voice low as I spoke to him.

SHORT STACK

"David. Walker knows who you are?"

He gave me a sly smile when he answered me. "You have to give Walker a little credit, Short Stack. He has a good sense about things. There weren't no fooling him. He's known about me for awhile. We have talked and he knows the whole story. He also knows if something should happen to me, there'd be a good chance you would lose your home with no father or husband around. I told you a long time ago Walker is a mite sweet on you. He will do whatever is necessary to protect you. Try not to be so hard on him."

I was dumbfounded, not knowing how I felt about Walker, or him knowing our secret. Obviously, Walker had not revealed to his blue-coat brother that David was actually my uncle, not my Pa. David had been going out of his way to convince me Walker would do us no harm, but was he right?

Further down the trail, Walker told me about "The Indian Removal Act." The Choctaw had already made the journey to the new land the white man called a reservation. It was a long journey to the reservation in the Oklahoma Territory, somewhere around eight hundred to a thousand miles, depending on the Indian tribe's original location. Along the way, many of the Indians, especially women, children and the elderly, died due to starvation, the bitter cold weather and disease, the weakest dying first. The Choctaw were driven from their homes with only the clothes on their backs—some with no moccasins on their feet or blankets to keep them warm. One by one, the Seminole, the Creek and the Chickasaw Indians had all been forced to leave their homes and move to this place called a reservation. Their homes, possessions and crops were all burned, anything of value stolen.

The Cherokee was the last tribe to make the journey to the Oklahoma Territory. The forced march of the Indians took six months. They traveled by foot, by horse, by wagon, or steamboat to reach their destination, and one out of every four Indians died on this journey. The unmarked graves along the Trail of Tears told the story of death for the Indian tribes.

I reckon Pa was right: "Wealth and land goes to a body's head faster than a jack rabbit with a hound dog hot on its heels."

CHAPTER 16
Ross' Landing

We had been on the trail for six days, and tempers were running a mite short. Bullet had finally lost Adahy's scent after the first hard rain, but there were still signs of the soldiers' horses and the wagons. There were many footprint tracks left behind by the Cherokee carved into the Tennessee earth after the hard rain, and they were far too many too count. The small footprints of the young children tore me up the most. I wanted to save them all, but knew I couldn't.

We heard tell the soldiers were herding the Indians like cattle toward Ross' Landing on the Tennessee River, a six or seven day journey, depending on the weather and conditions of trail and travel. Ross' Landing was simple enough, consisting of a small trading post along with a rope ferry. For a half-dime, a horse and rider could load up on to the ferry and cross to the other side of the river. After your fare had been paid, you walked your horse onto a wooden flat boat being pulled across the water by ropes connected to the other side of the river. The ferry carried supplies such as furs, traps, ammunition, dried goods, grain, rice and beans to the other side of the river for settlers, soldiers and trappers.

A steamboat waited at Ross's Landing to carry the Indians down river to Decatur, along with about a half dozen flatboats. When they reached Decatur, the next part of their journey took them to Tuscumbia by iron horse. The last leg of their journey would be afoot, if they lived long enough to make their destination. Inside the railroad cars, the Indians were jammed together so tight disease rapidly spread. Everything inside of me screamed: *What the bloody hell! This is the Land of Milk and Honey? This is freedom? Where is the freedom for the Cherokee?* I had such a bad taste in my mouth for my own kind—it just wasn't right.

It was late fall by the time we reached Ross' Landing, and the turning leaves showed the early frost of winter blowing in the wind. Walker, David and I were in accord after talking it over a spell. We would ride into the Landing's trading post to find out what the folks were chewing the fat on. Walker and David tried to talk Waya and his warriors into staying put until we came back from the Landing, but they didn't cotton to sitting still. They allowed how there was no honor in a warrior doing nothing. Waya came right out with it: he and his men would do some scouting around on the outskirts of the settlement, while we were at the trading post.

Innocent-like, Walker and David chewed the fat with trappers, travelers, and some of the local folk. I kept quiet, for I didn't feel like I could keep a civil tongue in my head. Walker, curse his hide, without a doubt found out more helpful information than I could have, simply due to the fact that it was menfolk doing the jawing. The smile on his handsome face clearly showed his confidence in determining the truth from the gossip and tall tales. We did our level best to separate the wheat from the chaff, whether folks were spreading rumors, spinning a good yarn, or relating information that was truly useful.

There were three regiments of soldiers, and depending on the manpower available, each regiment could have anywhere from two hundred and fifty soldiers to five hundred soldiers. It was neither here nor there, as we knew we were up against a mountain of soldiers who had been dispatched to guard the flow of the nearly four thousand Cherokee Indians being relocated to the Oklahoma Territory. The regiments were spread out on along the predetermined route the Indians traveled. There was clearly more unarmed Cherokee than soldiers, but none of the women and children, or the elderly, could fight back. If there were warriors among them, they were without weapons. The soldiers had made sure all weapons had been confiscated, including knives, rifles, bows and arrows, even sticks and stones.

The first group of around eight hundred Indians had already been loaded onto flat boats and a ferry then floated downriver under the watchful eyes of the soldiers of the 51st Regiment. The second group of Indians was to embark down river in a couple of days following the first, once the boats had returned, or new ones had arrived. Walker and I bought the supplies we needed, food and ammunition, and then we rode back to camp.

After we all talked it over, it was decided we'd wait and see if any of the family we were looking for might be among the second group to leave. It would be like finding a needle in a haystack, but there was no point in us going forward if the family we were looking for was behind us, and with us being on horseback, we could travel much faster than the Indians on foot. We had to backtrack a day's journey to intercept the next group of Indians before they reached Ross' Landing.

I was mighty fidgety. I wanted to find Adahy. It

SHORT STACK

didn't take us long to find the second group of Indians behind us, and I wanted desperately to find the boy I was looking for. In so many ways, I had raised Adahy, giving him everything I wanted my brothers to have: a warm fire, a home, and love, along with the knowledge and strength of character to survive on the mountain.

I climbed down from my horse and pulled out the shirt Adahy had worn. I took in a deep breath with my face buried in his shirt, and in my mind's eye, I could see him, and I could smell him. Nervously, I once again held in my hands the garment Adahy had been wearing before he had been taken. We circled around the group of soldiers and Indians, careful not to draw attention to ourselves. If Adahy was in this throng of Indians, Bullet was damn sure to find him. I just knew it, for the scent in the garment was still strong.

As quiet as we could, Walker and I shadowed Bullet along the wooded outskirts of the trail the marching Indians and soldiers had traveled. I felt sick inside from fretting, and I really wanted to ride through the crowd of Indians crying and screaming Adahy's name, but I knew that would only cause more trouble than we could handle, and I refused to let Walker see my weakness.

I called Bullet with the low whistle of a bobwhite quail that always brought him to me.

Once again, I prayed silently as I held out the garment for Bullet to smell. I ruffled his ears, softly petting him as he sniffed the shirt, and then I said over and over again, "Bullet, find Adahy. Come on boy, you can do it. Bullet, find Adahy!" Bullet understood me better than folks, and he took off like a shot.

If the soldiers eyed us and became suspicious then we'd allow that we had just been out hunting, our dog was trailing game, and got separated from us. Walker didn't like coming out in the open none, but he had given up trying to make me do anything. I, in turn, had learned to follow his lead in certain situations. So when he spoke, I did listen.

"Short Stack, if'n we find Adahy, don't you go throwin' a fit! Don't do nothing to let anyone see you know him. If'n we are lucky enough to find him, Adahy will know we are here, and he will be ready for whatever happens. He might even be able to tell us if Waya's wife and son are in this group or the first."

I looked at Walker and nodded my head in agreement. "Walker, we don't always see eye to eye on things, but I am grateful." He smiled at me, and I fell silent for a few moments.

"Hell, let's ride."

Bullet followed the trail, I could tell he was becoming more excited as we rode along—he had picked up Adahy's scent. When Bullet bolted into the woods, I was praying with all my heart that he was on the right trail. We rode up on the soldiers, who did not appear to be at all friendly. One of the soldiers in front of the regiment raised a hand to stop the column of Indians and soldiers as Bullet ran past him. We were on Bullet's heels as Walker whoaed up and spoke first to the soldier with fancy stripes on his uniform sleeves, who appeared to be charge of the marching horde. He was a stern-looking older gent with gray hair, cold blue eyes, and his jaw was set tight with pure arrogance.

"Morning, sir," Walker said, touching the brim of his hat. "Looking for our hunting dog. We have been trailing some game, and I think all these folks got him a mite worked up. Don't want no trouble—just want to get my best hunting dog back. My girl here is not about to leave our dog, and I don't want no trigger itching soldiers taking a shot at my girl over a dog."

Walker looked at him with no expression of emotion on his face. The soldier studied Walker a moment and surely believed him as he nodded his head in accord. Walker turned and looked at me like he wanted to tan my hide. "Girl, we got no business here—go find that damn dog and let's be on our way!"

The soldiers began to laugh, and my blood was

boiling. Walker had enjoyed his play-acting a little too much, but I made fast tracks after Bullet. I would seek my revenge on Joe Walker later.

I was moving along the outside of the group of Indians, carefully scanning their faces, when I finally spotted Adahy. My heart leapt into my throat—Bullet had brought me straight to him. He looked fence rail-thin, half-starved, cold and tired, but I could not do what my heart screamed to do with unending waves of pain and grief.

I wanted to run to him, hold him, and scream with everything I had inside of me: "Adahy, its Short Stack! I'm here! You're safe now!"

And then start shooting. But Walker had given me a stern warning against such foolishness. Why did that man always have to be right? I had no choice but listen to him, whether I liked it or not.

Bullet jumped all over Adahy, and as I pulled him away from Adahy, I said, "Sorry, boy. My dog here was chasing deer, but got plumb side-tracked, so looks like rabbit stew and wild onions over on the east ridge tonight."

A couple of soldiers noticed the commotion and rode up on us. The two soldiers wasn't shy about listening to me talk, so I quickly spoke up and looked at them with fear in my eyes, pulling Bullet back behind me with a rope loosely looped around his neck.

SHORT STACK

"Indians don't eat dogs, do they sir?"

The soldiers chuckled with amusement, wide smiles graced their lips with laughter. Shaking their heads from side to side they quickly moved on showing overconfidence and authority.

I whispered to Adahy, "Fall back as best you can. Slip away when you catch wind of something going on just before Ross' Landing. You watch for a sign now, you hear?"

Adahy nodded his head in accord, letting me know he understood with sad eyes that shone now with a glimmer of hope. I rode slowly away with Bullet persistently pulling on his rope, desperately trying to stay with Adahy. I know, Bullet must have been real confused, as I dragged him away from Adahy. He had found what I had sent him after, but then I had turned around and left Adahy behind. Walker was still talking to the soldier in the fancy uniform when I rode up with Bullet.

Walker exploded with laughter. "Did you happen to find that eight-point buck your old hound was tracking?"

I didn't cotton to his laughter or the smart remark, so I thought up one of my own. "No *Pa*, I'm sorry, all these Indians probably scared the livin' daylights out of that buck. Maybe we should try a little closer to the river. If'n we don't kick up a rabbit, we could try fishing for our supper."

Sharon A. Cantor

Walker tipped his hat to the soldier, and we rode off in the opposite direction of our camp. Once we were on the trail, and out of earshot, Walker had to ask: "What was all that 'Pa' stuff?"

"Well, you are getting a few grey hairs Walker, and I wanted to be respectful in front of the soldier so he believed we were kin."

"Horse hockey!"

His comment tickled my fancy, and I really wanted to laugh out loud, but somehow I managed to hold it inside. In silence, Walker and I scouted out the lay of the land in every direction before we finally returned to our camp. Waya was excited we had found Adahy, but he was disappointed that we had no word on the whereabouts of his wife and son.

Before the sun crested in the sky, we were once again following what was becoming known in these parts as the Trail of Tears. It was almost midday when a horse unexpectedly stampeded 'accidentally on purpose' through the crowd of Indians and soldiers. In the confusion, Adahy was able to slip far enough away from the others for Walker to reach him and pull him up onto the back of his horse then disappear into the woods. Walker was careful and took his time bringing Adahy back. I had already begun to panic and was getting ready to light out of camp to look for them when Walker

SHORT STACK

finally rode up. I jumped off my horse and ran to Adahy, no longer having to keep my emotions inside of me.

A passel of tears streamed down my face as I hollered, "Adahy! Adahy!" I turned my attention to Joe Walker. "Walker, was you followed?"

When I glanced at Walker, I was taken back—I had never seen him ever look so worn and tired as he climbed down off his horse. Walker set right down on the ground and took a long, deep breath, as Adahy began to speak.

"No, I don't believe anyone is trailing us. I had been waiting for a chance to get away, Short Stack, when you showed up. There were too many of us for the soldiers to keep track of. Some of the soldiers did not know how to read or write, and they were shy about admitting it, so many of our names were never written down, and they don't know exactly how many of us they were guarding."

Walker sat quietly on the ground, listening to Adahy's words. By the time Adahy had finished talking, there was no doubt Walker was madder than a scalded bullfrog. He rose slowly to his feet, pulling his long knife for its scabbard as he stood. I froze with fear as he walked up behind Adahy with the knife in his hand and rage in his eyes.

Walker grabbed a handful of Adahy's long black hair, yanking Adahy toward him. Within a heartbeat, Walker's knife sliced through the air, cutting off a considerable length of Adahy's long black hair, throwing it at my feet.

"Damn it, Short Stack! I told you to cut his hair a long time ago. It would have saved us all a right smart of grief."

I knew Walker was right, but I didn't have to like it, and my eyes reflected the fire of his words. "Walker, give me that knife. I need to clean up the mess you made."

Walker handed me the knife butt first then he walked over to his horse and rummaged through his saddle bags. It didn't take him long to find what he was looking for, he came back with a worn-out, brown floppy hat.

"Adahy should also keep his head covered after you clean up what you call my mess. His hair is black as night."

CHAPTER 17
Abandoned Cabins

Adahy was so hungry, and he looked painfully frayed around the edges. There had been little food given to the Indians along their journey along the Trail of Tears. I gave Adahy a small amount of beef jerky, and a cold biscuit with some water to wash it down. I promised him after a couple hours, I would give him more to eat. I just wanted to make sure he could hold it down.

The next task at hand was to clean up that butchery of a haircut Walker had given him as best I could. I had no choice but to cut Adahy's hair short. Without a doubt, Walker had made his point concerning the length of his hair. Walker, David and Waya were standing just off the clearing, talking amongst themselves with the other warriors.

I just knew that couldn't be good, so I up and asked them, "What are you all fixing to do? I know you're up to something, and since you're not chewing the fat with me, sure as a goose goes barefoot in the summertime, I know I'm probably not going to like it."

David gave me a stern look, and then shot Walker a sidelong glance. David ran his hand through his hair and then took a long, deep breath. "Before you get your dander up and go off all half-cocked, just hear us out Short Stack. We have found Adahy, and he is safe, but now that first group of Cherokee is way ahead of us, by at least a week. We got some hard ridin' to do. We want you to go back to the cabin with Adahy. It's already getting late in the season and snow will more than likely start falling before y'all make it back."

My feathers had sure enough been ruffled, and I could feel the hairs on the back of my neck stand straight up. "I've been on this journey a damn sight longer than either one of you. You're going to need every rifle you got and then some. Unless you have forgotten, I am a damn good shot. I won't slow you down none and neither will Adahy."

Walker quickly stepped up and took me gently by the shoulders. He gazed into my eyes with concern so genuine, it nearly took my breath away. "Short Stack, please don't take us the wrong way, especially not on my account. We know you can keep up with us, and we know you've a good eye for shooting. Look at me, girl. You have found

SHORT STACK

Adahy, now take him home and let us go after the others. We all need clear heads about us, and we can't do that frettin' about you or Adahy getting shot. You know as well as I do we can move faster without you, Short Stack, and we would feel a mite better about things if'n we didn't have to keep looking over our shoulder to make sure you're all right. Hell girl, the journey home won't be easy sledding neither. It's going to be mighty rough, you're going to have to do some hunting along the way for food, and you will have to stay clear of soldiers or Indians stragglers that the soldiers might be tracking. After we find Waya's family we will meet back up with you at the cabin. Let Adahy get a good night's sleep, and let him eat his fill, if'n he can keep the food down. By first light, I–we—want you on the trail towards home."

I didn't like it, but I knew Walker was right. I didn't want to risk losing Adahy again. He was still very weak and looked plumb pinched, but he had managed to keep his food down, so I gave him more beef jerky, dried peaches and biscuits. I didn't sleep well that night. I couldn't quite put my finger on what was bothering me the most. Whether it was the dangerous miles I was about to travel headed back to the mountain or leaving Walker behind, knowing full well what he was riding into. I wasn't sure, but at the crack of dawn, we parted ways. I hugged David, but when I turned toward Walker, words just failed me. I looked into his eyes that showed only concern, and there was no sign of that big, dumb grin.

I really wanted to hug him too, but all I could muster as I mounted my horse was to say, "Walker, you take care, you hear?"

"I will. You do the same, Short Stack."

With that said, Walker slapped my horse on the rump, and we were off. Adahy and I stayed away from the main mountain trail, but kept close sight of it, so we knew we were headed in the right direction toward home. David had been right. There weren't a lot of leaves left on the trees, which meant less cover for us. We had to be right careful to steer clear of folks. You could feel it in the air—there would be an early snow on the mountain. The seasons came and went as they pleased, and a body just dealt with the mountains' fickle nature.

We had been riding for a couple of days, and our food was beginning to run low. I let Bullet roam a little, hoping he would chase up a rabbit. Bullet had to sniff around much more than usual, as the hunting was scarce.

Toward nightfall with the shadows fading, Bullet took off running like he was scalded. Adahy and I rode after him, hoping for a warm supper that

SHORT STACK

night. We rode into a small grove of trees with four cabins, built almost side by side. I didn't know what to make of the cabins. There were no horses or livestock around. There was nothing but an eerie silence. We saw no sign of life, no sound of folks—it was as quiet as judgment day.

Out of the corner of my eye, I caught movement. Adahy picked up on it straight away, and after looking at each other, nodding our heads, we pulled our rifles and quietly dismounted. After roping off our horses, cautiously we walked up to the cabin, where someone had just closed the front door. Carefully, Adahy and I stood on each side of the doorway of the cabin, I opened the door and announced out arrival.

"Is anybody about? Don't mean you no harm."

A little girl with long red hair and freckles to match, peeked her head around the corner of the wood pile beside the fireplace. Softly, she said, "Our folks ain't come back."

"My name is Short Stack, and this here is my son Adahy. What is your name?"

Softly, the little girl murmured, "Suzy."

"Where did your folks go?"

"We had us some trouble. Folks was shootin' at us."

"Adahy, check the other cabins. Scout around and see what you can find. I am going to light a fire and warm the cabin. Whoever else was livin' here is long gone."

As soon as Adahy left the cabin, two other children came out of their hiding places. Suzy looked to be the oldest, around eight or nine years old. The other two children looked to be four or five years old—one a boy, the other a girl. All three children just stood and watched me as I built a fire, but as soon as the blaze was dancing high in the fireplace, all three gathered round to warm themselves, without saying a word.

When Adahy came back, his face was stern. He lowered his voice to keep the children from hearing his words. "Found some bodies on the south side of the cabins. All of them were scalped Short Stack, but I don't believe it was by Indians. The other cabins were ransacked. Whoever killed those folks took whatever they could find. I didn't find any horses, rifles or ammunition."

"We can't leave these young'uns here with no folks about. Go back to the other cabins and search for food, blankets, furs or even rugs. We need to build two sleds, one for the children to ride on and the other for whatever we can find to take with us. We have two strong horses and hopefully at a slower pace, the horses will be able to pull the load. I am goin' to take Bullet out for a run. Maybe with a bit of luck he will kick up a rabbit or two. A hot

SHORT STACK

meal of rabbit stew sounds mighty good right about now."

Suzy began to cry. "Please don't leave us."

Kneeling down in front of her, I wrapped my arms around her and softly told her, "Suzy, don't you fret none, girl. I am coming right back. Are you hungry? When did you eat last?"

"Day before yesterday, I think."

By this time, the other two children also ran to me, clinging onto me for dear life. The dam had broke, and all three children were crying, and wanted to be held and protected.

"Hush now, you are all safe. We won't leave you. Adahy and I just need to get busy and get some things done. Suzy, can you keep an eye on the other children for me?"

Suzy shook her head 'yes' and offered up the names of the other two children. "This is Katy and the boy here is Benjamin."

"Keep a lookout while I am hunting us up some supper. Adahy won't be far away. Just holler out as loud as you can, and he will make fast tracks for you. Just stay put by the fire and warm up while we are out and about. Adahy and I will be back as soon as we can. Adahy, bring back whatever you can find to this cabin. Come on, Bullet let's hope your ole nose can chase us up a couple of rabbits."

A light snow was on the ground, so I looked for

sign of tracks, but wasn't seeing much of anything. Then Bullet took off like a shot. I followed as close behind as I was able, but Bullet was a whole lot faster than me. In no time flat, I looked up to see Bullet heading back toward me, carrying a rabbit in his mouth, and I hadn't wasted nary a shot.

I patted his head with approval and hung the rabbit from my gun belt. "Good boy! We need one more. We have more hungry mouths to feed. Find me another rabbit, boy."

About that time, I heard the chattering of a squirrel sitting pretty in a barren maple tree not far from me. Bullet was excited and began barking at the squirrel as it chatted away. The squirrel was clearly giving us thunder for disturbing his slumber. I aimed my rifle and brought the squirrel down with one shot. I cleaned the meat and headed back up to the cabins. Adahy had already returned, but the children were happy to see me too. He had found some old blankets, several quilts, a few kettles to cook in, sugar, coffee and a bear rug.

Adahy and I were in agreement that Indians had not attacked these folks and neither had soldiers. Bad men on the mountain preyed on new settlers who wasn't used to this way of life or any sort of violence. Settlers were generally good-mannered folk, trusting a little too much to the wrong sort of people.

SHORT STACK

I put a kettle on with the rabbit and squirrel meat to cook over the fire and found some dried beans to add to the meat. While it cooked, Adahy and I went about the chore of making sleds. Adahy cut long limbs of an oak tree that we could tie off to the horses. Then we used smaller branches to cross the longer limbs to carry the supplies and the children. The bear skin fit right nice to cover the bottom of one of the sleds, and we used a heavy wool blanket to cover the bottom of the other one. The children would all ride bundled together on one sled, and body heat from each of the children would help them all stay warm. The bear skin and the wool blanket would provide a good layer for the children to sit on. All the supplies we had come across would be carried on the other sled, except the blankets and quilts, which would be wrapped around the children.

I made some biscuits to go with the stew, and all of us enjoyed a hot meal that night. I was a mite concerned about Katy. She had uttered not one word, not even when I tucked her in bed that night. Adahy and I both felt bad about their folks and the others who had died, but the ground was froze solid. There was no way for us to bury them proper. I had a mind to bring them inside and burn the cabin down as we left, but then again, I didn't want to attract any attention to us. Pulling two sleds, it would be easy to follow us in the light snow, so I thought better of burning the cabin. I didn't want us to be followed by anyone.

CHAPTER 18
Meet Your Maker

The next morning, we lit out at the crack of dawn. The children were a mite persnickety about the hour, but we had to pack up what clothes we could find for them and get a move on. With each passing day, the bitter cold wind of Old Man Winter was blowing snow down the mountain. We still had some difficult traveling to do, and time wasn't on our side. After a couple of days, the children were becoming more than a little restless. They were downright cranky, fussing at each other or whining about their cramped ride. They were warm enough and while the grub might not be the best—and cold to boot—at least we *had* food, and that was all I cared about at the moment.

I could understand how the young'uns felt, but there was nothing I could do about it. It was going to be a long ride with few stops, so when they grumbled some about the tough beef jerky and cold biscuits, I had to firmly tell them, "Stop all that caterwauling. Indians, soldiers or bad folks can hear y'all for a country mile. It's all we got. If'n you're eating, least I won't have to listen to all your jawing, so shut up and eat!"

Adahy and I were keeping them alive and doing the best we could. Suzy and Benjamin could like it or lump it, but at least they would be alive to tell the tale. Little Katy did not utter one word.

Whenever we found good cover from the wind, we would hold up at nightfall to sleep for a few hours, not daring to build a fire. Before the sun would grace the sky, we were moving again.

On the third day out, we came across a rickety old wooden bridge. After talking it over with Adahy, we made up our minds about that old wooden rope bridge. We didn't want to chance trying to cross the old bridge. It just didn't appear sturdy enough to withstand the weight of the horses and the sleds. The bridge appeared to have several missing wood planks, and the ones that remained were weathered with age, just like the frayed old ropes. We just couldn't risk it with the children. The weather was cold enough now to freeze the river in some of the more shallow parts, so we decided to travel upriver until we found a

SHORT STACK

solid place to cross over on the ice.

We needed to fill our canteens with water, so we made our way down to the river's edge. We huddled beneath the cover of the bridge to block the wind, so we could also eat some cold biscuits as we refilled the canteens. The water along the shoreline was frozen, so a body had to take care when walking out onto the ice, making sure the ice would hold under the weight of your body while you filled your canteen. I was just about done filling the last canteen when the ice beneath me began to quiver. My heart skipped a beat as I glanced back at Adahy.

I lowered my voice and used hand signals to convey my words. "Take the horses into the cover of them trees and tie them off. A good many horses are headed this way."

Adahy had also felt the ground tremble beneath him, and his young face could not mask his concern. He made fast tracks for the horses, as I made my way off the ice. I slightly raised my voice as I ran up behind him. "Hurry!"

There were large boulders and rocks along the river's tree line, giving us plenty of cover. I had to keep the children calm and quiet without scaring the living daylights out of them. I told them in a calm whisper, "You all need to be as quiet as a l'il mouse in church. We need to let them soldiers pass right on by us, no matter what you hear, stay put right here and don't let out a peep. Adahy and I will be right close just a stone's throw down by the river. Suzy, please keep'em quiet as best you can."

I pressed a finger gently to my lips as I backed away from the children. I slowly made my way back down to the boulders along the river bank where Adahy was waiting. I looked over the edge of the boulders, and I saw soldiers approaching that rickety old bridge. Adahy signaled to me with two fingers pointing toward his eyes then pointing at the soldiers.

The soldier in the front raised his hand high into the air, and then clenched his fingers into a tight fist and held it there. The column of soldiers behind him slowed their horses and pulled up to a stop.

From where I was sitting, and near I could tell, the fancy-looking soldier at the front was talking to a couple of men dressed in brown buckskin clothing. The two men in buckskin were waving their arms in the air, pointing at the bridge and without a doubt was having a heated chat regarding the bridge. Slowly, they began backing their horses up, shaking their heads *no*, refusing to cross the bridge.

The next thing I recollect was the fancy soldier

SHORT STACK

ordering the other soldiers to follow him across the bridge. There was just a few soldiers at first, but then they began to move a little faster across the bridge. Halfway across the bridge, one of the horses bolted, vaulting high into the air, coming down with the full weight of the horse and rider onto the old wooden planks. The front legs of the horse broke through the planks beneath his hooves and struggled wildly to find freedom.

There was no calming this horse down, for it was trapped like a fly in a spider's web. The other horses sensed his fear and began acting up as well, dancing into the air and coming down hard, the full force of their hooves pounding against the old bridge. The bridge began to sway wildly, cracking and snapping in several places until finally, it just came apart. The soldiers and their horses were falling into the icy river below with an outburst of screams and splashes.

The soldiers who had been able to control their horses and remain on the river bank watched in horror as their comrades fell into the frigid water. Immediately, they pulled ropes from their saddles and began chasing the soldiers and horses being swept downstream. If the river-bound soldiers survived the fall without having the wind knocked out of 'em, they still had to keep enough good sense about themselves to grab a rope. If they still had hold of a horse, they had to hang on for dear life and pray that horse wanted out of the freezing river just as bad as they did. In that bitter cold water, they only had a few minutes to make it to shore before the icy water would numb their limbs, confuse their minds, and then finally claim their lives.

I couldn't help but recall the memory of a deer that I had come across last winter, down along the river bank. The deer had fallen through the ice and no matter how the deer struggled, he could not get solid footing enough to set himself free. I know it was just a deer, but I felt a mite poorly for the unfortunate animal that was frozen plumb solid, hard as a rock, hung up halfway out of the iced up river. I never forgot the look of fear and hopelessness in that deer's large, dark brown eyes.

I spoke softly. "Adahy, we have got to get out of here. Let's go upstream and find a place to cross in the shallows." It was clear as spring water that our reckoning about that old bridge from the beginning had been right.

It took us the better part of an hour—maybe just a tad longer—creeping quietly along the river's edge, before we found us a shallow place in the river to cross over. It had to be frozen enough to bear the weight of a horse and a sled. I felt so proud of Adahy when he insisted on testing

SHORT STACK

the crossing first under his own weight. After he walked across the frozen shallows with no problem, he came sliding back across the icy surface and led his horse across, tying him off on the other side.

Adahy returned, quickly harnessing the supplies he carried on the sled, and he pulled the sled across. I untied the sled from my horse, secured the children with a reassuring smile and Adahy pulled the children across. It was then my turn, and I walked softly, listening for any sign of the ice cracking, but I safely reached the other side of the river with my horse. I grabbed ahold of Adahy and hugged him so tight, he chuckled out loud, even as I cried tears of joy and pride.

As soon as we had crossed over the river, Adahy and I began recognizing the lay of the land. While we were still a good sight further away than a stone's throw from home, we were surely closer as the crow flies. It made me feel some better to be in familiar surroundings. We had several hours of daylight left, so we kept moving.

I knew where there was a small cave to be found, and we could reach it by nightfall if we pushed forward at a little faster pace. I told Adahy to keep a good lookout for game. If we managed to hunt something down, we could build a fire in the cave to warm our bones and cook up some meat for the children.

Just when I was about to give up hope we would have hot vittles for supper, we stumbled onto a turkey. Adahy was a tad faster on the trigger than me when the turkey flew up into the air. He brought that bird down, and I was downright pleased as pie, knowing we were going to have a hot meal for supper.

Birds are a little harder to clean than deer, rabbit or even squirrels, but I didn't mind plucking them feathers, not the least little bit. First thing, I had to put on a kettle full of water on over a roaring fire to boil. Next, I lopped off the turkey's head and hung the bird upside down long enough for the bird to bleed out. I didn't want the young'uns to see the turkey bleed out, so I took it a-ways off from the mouth of the cave to complete this task.

Once this was done, I carefully plunged the bird into the boiling water, holding onto the bird by the feet. After a few minutes in the boiling water, it was feather-plucking time! After the feathers had been removed, I cut them ugly feet off, and commenced to cooking. Once safely inside the cave, Adahy and I took turns roasting the turkey over an open fire and tending to the children. I declare, that turkey smelled like heaven

SHORT STACK

as it roasted over the open fire. All of us was more than just a mite hungry, resembling a pack of old black bears waking up after a long winter of sleeping. The first thing them old bears eat is going to taste mighty good.

I used up the last of the flour we had with us, but it gave me a full pan of biscuits, enough to last another day. I watched them biscuits mighty close after I sat them in the fire. I didn't want to burn them biscuits. The food smelled so good, I hoped it would not bring any varmints to us, looking for supper.

As we got closer to the cabin, Adahy and I decided to hunt for bigger game. I had dried fruit and vegetables at the cabin—I put them up every year—but there was no meat hanging in the smokehouse. When I left, I had not known when, or even if I would be coming back. On the mountain, you only kill the animals you plan on having for supper.

In two days, we would be home. It was cold enough now to freeze any game we were lucky enough to come across. After they were field-dressed and ready for cooking, we would put them in the snow at night and rope them behind the horses during the day to keep the meat frozen. The only real danger was bigger game—like a hungry mountain lion—following your kill, until the meat was frozen solid. The scent of fresh blood would hang in the air for them to pursue.

Under the circumstances, the children all seemed to be holding up well, except for Katy. It bothered me some that she had not spoken a solitary word—hadn't uttered neither a cry nor even a whimper. If she was really afraid, Katy would cling to me, but she never uttered a peep and no emotion ever showed on her tiny face.

We feasted on turkey and hot biscuits. Everyone ate their fill, and we felt safe and warm. When the children were finally sleeping, it was a downright peaceful feeling watching them sleep in the shadows that danced off the walls of the cave in the firelight. Maybe that was why I had a fidgety feeling in my gut—everything was just going *too* perfect. Adahy could read me like a book. He knew something was bothering me, before I even said a word to him.

"You get some sleep," I said quietly. "I'll wake you in a few hours. I got a feeling deep down in my bones. We need to keep an extra good lookout tonight."

Adahy dozed off, and I kept the fire going with some dried-out branches we had gathered. I was just about to wake Adahy for his watch, when I heard an odd sound. Maybe it was someone stepping on a twig, maybe it was just an animal in the brush, or maybe it was the fire crackling, but I sat up and took notice.

I tugged on Adahy's left moccasin to wake him, and then I quickly put my finger to my lips. He sat up straight away and grabbed his rifle. Nervously, we looked at each other in the firelight, both holding our breath, waiting for another sound. When we heard the faint sound of footsteps crunching on the snow, we held our rifles a little tighter.

A couple of minutes later, a man as big as a full-grown bear stepped into the entrance of the cave. I noticed straight away that even a matted old bear would have looked a damn sight prettier. I did not hesitate, I pulled Pa's rifle to my shoulder and dropped the big man right where he stood, the rifle's sharp report thundering along the cave walls. Whoever was with him made fast tracks, leaving him to his own fate. There is no honor amongst thieves.

"I promise Pa, though I walk through the valley of the shadow of death, I will fear no evil. I know I promised you he would dangle from a mountain rope, but without a rope, I made do! Pa, that ugly bastard met his maker just the same."

CHAPTER 19
Answered Prayer

I had to calm the children down, as they were considerable riled up from the rifle fire. Benjamin and Suzy screamed like banshees, but Katy just sat on her bedroll, rocking slowly back and forth, seeming to be oblivious to all the chaos and danger taking place around her. Once Suzy and Ben had finally settled down and drifted back to sleep, Adahy took a quick look around outside the cave. The dead man's horse wandered right up to Adahy like he had known him his whole life. In the saddlebags, Adahy found a pistol with ammunition, and a scarred up old Winchester rifle riding alongside the saddle in the scabbard. The vulture had a small buckskin money bag attached to his belt with a couple of coins in it. I would make good use of those coins.

Even dead, I felt only hate for the man who I saw with my own eyes kill my Pa with a smile on his evil, ugly face. That bastard had a hand in torturing my Ma, my sisters—maybe even murdered them, so you could easy bet, I didn't worry none about burying that piece of horse dung. As far as I was concerned, the critters could have at him. I wanted with all my heart to find Ma's gold locket, but I figured it was long gone.

Early the next morning we moved on, and we kept moving even after the shadows began to fall at dusk and long into the night. We had to put distance between us and any other men who might be trying to track us down for killing one of their own. If nothing else, maybe trailing us just to finish what they had started. The closer we got to the cabin, the more I could feel the bitter cold wind down in my bones, as it was blowing down the mountain. The snow started to fall slowly at first, and then picked up, swirling around us, pretty as a picture, but a fair sight more dangerous. The freezing wind blew without mercy and drifted the snow higher and higher. We were a within a day's ride of the cabin, but we had to hold up and look after the children. Without a doubt, the horses also needed a rest, for if'n we lost even one horse, we would most likely freeze

SHORT STACK

to death. We had been pushing ourselves hard to reach the warmth and safety of the cabin. The children needed to be fed a good, hot meal and they needed the warmth of a roaring fire to take the chill off their bones.

Adahy and I both agreed we would stop at White Box Gorge for the night. Between the cliffs of the gorge, there would be shelter from the snow and bitter cold wind. We were all dog-tired by the time we reached the gorge. Adahy had done some scouting ahead of us and had brought down a five point-buck. When I caught up to him, he was skinning out the buck. I was plumb tickled to see the meat. Now we would have a hot meal and plenty of meat to haul up to the cabin. While Adahy finished dressing out the meat, I moved on up through the valley and found a safe place to camp, then I began searching for firewood.

By the time Adahy came riding into camp with the venison, I had a fire burning fiercely, and the flames danced along the walls of the sandstone bluffs towering over us. I had hauled enough wood into our rock shelter to last us through the night. I filled the kettle up plumb full of snow and melted the icy snow over the fire then I filled our canteens with hot water, sliding them under our bedrolls, so they would not freeze during the night. I melted more snow in the kettle and added a nice cut of meat Adahy had sliced off the venison for our supper. I poured the last of the dried beans into the kettle, along with a couple of wild onions.

Adahy and I took turns keeping watch, looking around outside, but the night proved to be calm. As the meat cooked over the open fire, we could almost taste it, as all of us were hungry, our mouths watering with the sweet smell of food. Nobody cottoned to the meat being tender if that meant waiting much longer, so when we ate it, it was a shade on the tough side, but it filled our bellies. There was just no waiting for the meat to cook up tender.

By the morning light, we had a second wind about us, having rested up for the last leg of our journey. This day would prove to be the roughest, and our ragged little group crawled slowly up the mountain with the wind blowing fiercely in our faces, nearly blinding us with the white fury of snow.

There was no choice to be made. We had to keep going. There would be no stopping now until we reached the safety of the cabin. Just when I thought we would all be safe soon enough, my heart skipped a beat when I noticed the grey cloud of smoke curling up against the white snow drifting across the Tennessee sky.

SHORT STACK

"Hellfire! Someone is in the cabin!" I said aloud, more to myself than anyone else.

I had no idea who might be sitting pretty in my cabin—it could be squatters, or it could be the men who had attacked us a few nights back. They could have moved faster and traveled right on by us, giving us a wide berth since they knew we were armed, and we would fight back.

I would not walk directly into trouble—Pa had taught me that lesson all too well. I needed to find out who was inside the cabin, without letting them know what sort of trouble they had to deal with. The best plan Adahy and I could come up with was to send Bullet up to the cabin, drawing out whoever was inside. Seeing who might be afoot, checking out a barking dog, would at least give us an inkling of what we were up against. We had to get the children inside the cabin, but first we had to know who or what we were dealing with before sashaying through the cabin's front door.

I sat Bullet down and stroked him softly along his back, petting his head and scratching his ears. It was hard sending Bullet in, not knowing exactly what I was sending him into. I loved him dearly, but I knew there was no choice. I had to get Bullet excited enough to bark and play, but at the same time, I felt like I was betraying him.

"Bullet, we're home, boy! Watch'em, boy!

Get'em, boy!" I swatted the top of my leg several times and Bullet began to jump up and down, beginning to bark with excitement. I raised my voice. "Bullet, we're home, boy! Watch'em, boy! Get'em, boy!"

Bullet took off like a hot round toward the cabin, barking and carrying on like he was facing a pack of wolves. He dashed all the way to the front of the cabin, and then he stopped still, standing his ground. He moseyed forward a bit, finally stopping a couple yards from the front door of the cabin, looked back at me and continued to bark. The barking did not go unnoticed. A young boy opened the front door, followed closely behind by a woman I reckoned must have been his Ma. Even from a distance, I could tell she was older than me by a few years. I breathed a sigh of relief. Squatters, I knew, would be much easier to deal with than the trappers.

I asked Adahy to hold back with the children, while I went up to the cabin with the one sled carrying the venison, just to check things out. I knew there was no meat in the smokehouse, and there was no telling how long the folks had been in the cabin. They just might be in need of food, and we needed to be warm inside that cabin.

I stepped out from the trees and walked my horse and sled up to the cabin. The woman looked

SHORT STACK

at me and instantly froze. She didn't move even as I smiled at her.

"Howdy, my name is Short Stack. I want to thank you for getting my old cabin warm for me. It's a mite cold out this time of year. I brought back some venison, and I'll need to put it up in the smokehouse to cure some first. You all run into some kind of trouble?"

The woman ran from the cabin toward me so fast that I thought she would run right over the top of me. "Please, sweet Lord, can you get a bullet out? Some god-awful men attacked us, and they shot my husband. Please, can you get a bullet out? God help me! I don't know what to do!"

Her tears turned into breathless sobs, and I put my arms around her shoulders for comfort and hugged her. I signaled for Adahy by waving my hand, motioning for him over her shoulder to bring the children on up to the cabin. I walked her back toward the cabin with her boy right close behind us, and I eased her gently back inside the cabin door. The cabin looked just the same as I had left it—except for the man laying astraddle of my bed.

I stripped off my coat, rolled up my sleeves, and I asked her, "What's your name, ma'am?"

"Jenny."

"Jenny, there's a big ole kettle right over there.

I am going to need some boiling water. Fill that old kettle up with snow and put it over the fire. Are you wearing a petticoat?"

Jenny was horror-struck, but nodded her head yes. I handed her my knife and instructed her to cut the petticoat into strips about six inches wide for bandages. By then, Adahy had reached the cabin, after securing the horses and bringing up the children.

I called out to him. "Adahy, I need your help! Hurry, this man has been shot. He's lost a lot of blood. I have to get the bullet out, and I will need your help holding him down.

"Jenny, while we are helping him, gather the children—they need to be fed. Adahy brought up some venison and I've got dried vegetables in that wooden barrel over there, but first we need to get water on to boil so we can help him. What's his name?"

"John. John Mills. He's my husband. Oh, those horrible, god-awful men." Jenny broke down once again and the tears quickly flowed down her face, so I started giving orders.

"*Adahy*, put some snow in a kettle directly over the fire to melt and bring it to a boil."

"*Jenny*, get to cutting up them bandages. Take off that petticoat and don't be shy about doing it."

"*Suzy*, warm the children in front of the fire

and keep an eye on them until Jenny can help you."

"*Adahy*, once you get that kettle over the fire bring in more wood for the fire."

John Mills had lost a lot of blood, but that bullet had to come out. While Adahy and I worked on her husband, Jenny went from one task to the next, and it seemed to calm her down some having something to do. Once I had the bullet out, only time would tell if he was strong enough to survive. It would have hurt like hell if John had been conscious. Walker was much better than I at removing a bullet.

John slept fairly sound, and there was no fever. Since the bleeding had stopped, I figured he had a good chance at making it. The bullet had hit him in the right shoulder and lodged between the muscle and bone. When his shoulder healed, only time—and the Grace of the Good Lord—would tell how much movement he would have in his shoulder.

Once things finally calmed down, everyone had a chance to take a breath and sit a spell, enjoy a hot cup of coffee or even fall asleep. Jenny told us they had been separated from the wagon train due to an outbreak of measles. Folks on the wagon train were dying, and many of the wagons had left the safety of the wagon train, striking out on their own, hoping they had not contracted the fever of the measles.

Jenny had put on some venison stew with the dried vegetables, and it smelled mighty good. She was keeping herself busy with making biscuits while Adahy brought in the blankets, quilts and whatever supplies we had left. He even carried in more firewood, stacking it next to the fireplace, and afterward hung the meat in the smokehouse.

The children were playing on the floor, and Bullet was dozed off in front of the fireplace. I was surprised to see Katy fast asleep alongside of Bullet on the bear rug with one arm around him. Jenny saved the rich broth from the stew for John, and we put it just outside the front door of the cabin in the snow to keep until John needed it. The broth would do him good.

Jenny had finally settled herself down, and all of the children were finally sleeping peacefully. She told us about the men who had attacked their wagon. John had fought them off with the aid of their son Elliott, who was a fair shot with a rifle. Unfortunately, John had been wounded, and Elliott had driven the wagon as far as he could in the ever drifting snow. When Elliott couldn't dislodge the wagon from the snow, he unhooked the horses, rigged up a piece of wood from the wagon. Then he tethered the makeshift sled to the

SHORT STACK

horses to pull his father on, while he and his mother walked alongside and guided the horses. As soon as they saw the cabin, they thought their prayers had been answered. All of their earthly belongings had been left behind them in the wagon, about two miles north of the cabin.

Adahy placed his hand gently over Jenny's hand resting on the table. He looked into her eyes thoughtfully, patting her hand as he began to speak. "When the snow calms down, and John gets back on his feet, we have a couple of sleds we can use to bring back whatever we can salvage from your wagon. Come spring, there's a good chance we can repair and save the wagon."

CHAPTER 20
Coming Home

The next morning, Jenny showed me how to make pancakes just right! I had been using the right amount of flour in the batter, but I found out I what I needed to do was blend in smaller amounts of flour to the mixture instead of just dumping the flour into the batter all at one time. Everyone ate their fill, and I was right proud of those pancakes.

John woke up from time to time, and he was holding his own. John wasn't awake long enough yet to sip some broth or talk much, so we let him sleep. There was some fever, but that was to be expected, considering his body was fighting off infection from his wound. Jenny kept a good watch over her husband, changing his bandages, and making sure the fever didn't burn any higher.

I enjoyed being back at the cabin, and with the

young'uns around, it felt like home again. The only things missing were my brothers—and my burnt pancakes. I wished my brothers could taste my pancakes now, without the lumps of flour and without them being burnt.

Adahy knew what needed to be done, and he commenced straight away to chopping more firewood, and he was already planning to get up early the next morning to go hunting. The meat hanging in the smokehouse wasn't enough to last us till the next full moon with eight hungry mouths to feed.

Adahy was every bit the young man I had raised him to be. After the loss of Hialeah, seemed both of us had been cut adrift for a spell. Adahy had been too young to remember much, but I had told him everything about his ma except the bad parts. He had grown up from a small boy to be his own man, and he filled my heart with love and pride.

John roused from his slumber the next day, on and off for longer periods of time, and he was finally able to speak with Jenny and Elliott. There was a different manner to Jenny. She was getting stronger and smiling a whole lot more. The children were a little cramped, but warm, well-fed and mostly comfortable. Come spring, we would just have to make a few more beds.

SHORT STACK

It was coming on the mid-day hour when I heard Adahy ride back up from hunting. I made fast tracks, heading outside to either welcome him back with encouraging words, if he came back empty handed, or give him a big pat on the back for the wild game he did find. The children were all screaming to go out with me and clinging onto me like kudzu vines in the springtime. I almost felt like I was talking to Bullet, holding up my hand, warning the children to stay put. None of the children had the proper clothes on to be running about in the cold.

"Stay. I will be right back. Stay."

I stepped outside of the cabin door, waving at Adahy as he walked toward me holding the reins of his horse in one hand and a trio of rabbits held by their hind legs in the other. A broad smile flashed across his face—I had seen Pa do the same thing many times. Seeing Adahy now in the same way made my heart soar. There wasn't a cloud in the sky on that day, but suddenly I heard the roar of thunder, and I felt the lightning strike.

Adahy was knocked forward toward me from the force of the bullet, and then he dropped straight away to his knees. His stunned eyes met mine, and I ran toward him, not caring about the flying bullets. I fell to my knees and gathered him into my arms. Adahy's eyes held my very soul, and he smiled at me through the blood and the pain. He softly whispered, "Ma…"

Adahy died right there in my arms.

I had walked out of the cabin without my rifle, thinking I had nothing to fear, and instead I had found death. With the heart of a wild banshee beating out of control, I screamed uncontrollably, not forming real words, only a high-pitched wail of grief.

I had sounded the alarm well enough, but I needed to gain enough control to scream real words. "Jenny! Elliott! Grab the rifles!"

I kept Adahy's horse between me and the bullets as I backed up to the door of the cabin. When I was in front of the cabin door, I hit the horse hard across his backside, sending him off running. Once inside, tears flowed down my face like a river, and I was wracked with painful sobs I tried—but failed—to keep it all inside. I thought that I had been strong enough to handle most anything, but now I felt broken like never before.

Jenny was frantic when I stumbled in the door, asking a storm of questions. "What happened? Where is Adahy? Are you hurt?"

I pushed Jenny away from me with both hands, and she stumbled backward with *What the hell?* written all over her face. Her eyes held only fear as I screamed at her, "Stop your caterwaulin', woman! I can't think with you jawing at me! Them bastards killed Adahy! Now I'm alone! I ain't got nothing left! Leave me be! Just leave me alone!"

I cried, I screamed, I sobbed—finally stopping long enough to wipe my face on the back of my buckskin sleeve. I still had my back against the inside of the cabin door, and that was not a right smart place to be sitting, but at the time, I hardly cared.

The men outside was whooping and hollering, but I was in a fog until Katy ran up to me and threw herself into my arms. She wrapped her tiny hands tightly around my neck. My gut reaction was to roll to the other side of the door with her, my body tucked closely around her and my arms holding on tight. I landed on top of her, sheltering her in my arms. When I looked down at Katy, I saw fear in those eyes so innocent and blue.

I could see tears welling up in her eyes as she whispered, "I don't think you're so short. You look plenty big enough to me."

Her tiny voice trembled with such a sweet innocence, a voice I had never heard before, and it shocked me into realizing there was still some fight left in me.

My voice was calm, measured, but without a doubt a little hoarse from all my hollering.

"Jenny, keep loading them rifles. Elliott, keep a good lookout on the east side of the cabin, I will cover the west side. Suzy, keep the children together on the other side of John's bed, and all of you stay put."

I picked up my rifle, listening carefully to the desperate voices yelling outside. "I know y'all can hear me in there! We need food and a warm fire. Let us in!"

I opened the cabin door just a crack and fired a blind shot, hoping it wasn't blind at all and screamed, "That wasn't real friendly killing my son! You best move on while you still can!"

"You know we can burn you out!"

"You can try, but then again, you can die trying!"

It was a standoff, and all we could do was wait. I didn't know how many men were outside the cabin, but it finally dawned on me that Elliott just might.

"Elliott, do you remember how many men attacked your wagon?"

"I know there were at least three, maybe four—Pa shot at least one of them."

It was then that I remembered what Joe Walker had said to me. *Varmints like that just multiply—for every man you take out, they add two.* What I wouldn't give to see Walker's dumb grin right about now. I had been so overwhelmed with taking care of the children, I hadn't given Walker or Waya much thought. I hoped they had fared well, and that Waya had managed to find his wife and son.

I had to stay focused on the problem at hand. We had five, maybe six hours of daylight left. If the trappers were going to make a move on us, it would likely be under the cover of darkness. The temperature outside would be falling quick, and the men would become even more desperate. I was hoping they wouldn't try to burn us out, but we were warm and fed, while they were cold and hungry. Both groups needed the cabin to survive, and the longer we held out, the more desperate they would become. The snow had stopped falling, but there was still plenty of snow on the ground and ice still draped the trees like funeral shrouds. I knew time wasn't on our side, and there would be no sleeping until this was over one way or the other.

I couldn't tell how much time went by before I heard, "It's getting mighty cold out here—a man could catch his death of cold."

The cards were on the table. I could feel it, and I could see it in my mind's eye. It seemed that every last thing I had ever loved was now only a lost and wanderin' ghost haunting my soul. John tried to get up, but he was just too weak. Elliott loaded his Pa's rifle and laid it on the bed next to him. I should have been scared to death, but I knew I wouldn't be until it was all over with. Now, I generally don't care to take action before I have thought things over for a spell, but sometimes a body is just forced to react.

The first bullet creased the west side of the cabin, startling the children, who screamed and cried out in fear. Jenny did her very best to calm them down. I fired off a shot at a fleeting shadow.

"Elliott, watch your side. They may try it next. Keep an eye on the cabin door. They may try to come busting right through it."

Sure enough, they fired a few rounds on the east side, and we returned fire. I ran to the east side and got off a round or two, but then came the lightning and thunder right through the cabin door. They bolted a horse through the cabin door and followed it with a fierce volley of gunfire. The horse held no rider, but the spooked animal had turned wild with fear, bucking and vaulting. The cabin clearly wasn't big enough for the horse, but as quickly as it had started, all became quiet as the horse finally got turned around and scrambled back out the way it had come in.

I glanced at Elliott, who was still standing and appeared unharmed. Then my attention turned to

SHORT STACK

Jenny, John and the children, who were all safe for the time being. A shadowy figure stepped into the doorway, with his rifle was pointed straight at Elliott.

"Drop your rifles! I will shoot him! Do it now!"

I knew one of us would be dead for sure if I didn't do as he ordered, but if I did drop my rifle, everyone in the cabin would surely die. Before I could react, before I could even blink, a rifle report sounded, the echo rebounding throughout the hills. The trapper had a stunned look on his face as he slowly fell to his knees, and then he slammed onto the floor face-first. When I looked back at the doorway, there was surely a sight for sore eyes standing there: Joe Walker.

"Joe!" I screamed! "Oh my God! Walker!"

Quickly, two men appeared behind him, both dressed in brown buckskin. Their long, unruly manes of hair were tousled and windblown, making it difficult to see their faces. Joe was downright proud of himself as he looked at me with that dumb grin of his that always told me he was up to some kind of mischief.

"I've traveled a far piece to bring you something, Short Stack. I know you've been looking for a couple boys who up and got themselves lost. Take a look at these here young men while I drag this varmint outside."

Moving like I was slogging hip-deep through molasses, I stepped toward them, stopping cautiously before the first young man. I took my hand and gently brushed the hair away from his face. My body trembled uncontrollably, and my voice came out as a whisper of wonder.

"Clinton?"

I grabbed the arm of the other young man.

"Catlin?"

Hot tears ran down my face as I grabbed hold of both of them, spinning in a circle as I hugged them, jumping up and down, but not letting go of my brothers until the sobs of joy and relief no longer controlled my body. My mind finally snapped back to the reality of the situation.

"Walker, there were other men outside."

Joe spoke up calmly. "There are no men outside this cabin who are breathing now."

I approached Walker, running my hands over his broad shoulders, gazing into his eyes with a heartfelt truth of emotion. Without even thinking about what I was doing, I jumped into his arms, and it felt like a bolt out the blue when he held on tight. "Why are you always here when I need you?"

Clinton and Catlin began laughing, grinning from ear to ear, but after a stern look from

SHORT STACK

Walker, both of them choked back their amusement, turning their attention back to the others. Everyone was fine and they knew it, but they needed an excuse to walk away.

Joe took my hand and led me outside the cabin, spinning me around to face him. For a moment, I thought *good Lord, what have I done now?* When I gazed up at him, I saw only tenderness in his eyes. But I could tell this was serious, as his jaw was set firm.

"Short Stack, I've always known you were as stubborn as a Missouri mule. I am a mountain man—no more, no less. I don't have much to offer. I got a lot of rough edges, but I'm forthright and I'm strong. You can count on me to take care of you, and I am a damn good shot with a rifle."

I couldn't seem to make heads nor tails of what Walker was saying to me—everything felt like it was happening all at once, swirling around me like a wild winter blizzard. My son, my heart and soul, Adahy lay dead on the frozen ground outside.

I wanted to ask my brothers what had happened to them. Where had they been? Were they hurt? I wondered if they really remembered me. I wanted to tell them everything, I wanted to scream, I wanted to cry—but instead, Joe pulled me into his arms and kissed me. I had never been kissed like that in my entire life, and my whole body felt like it was ablaze. The hairs on the back of my neck stood straight up, and my legs did not want to support the weight of my body.

When Walker finally turned me loose, he said, "Think on it some."

With a slight tug at the brim of his hat, Walker strode away from me, and he never looked back. I turned and walked back inside the cabin feeling more than a mite awkward, but instinct took over again in short order as I walked back inside. Jenny had calmed down the children and tended to John so he would lay still. My brothers stood before me, standing tall and strong as pine trees, and I was downright proud of 'em.

I learned it had indeed been the Kiowa who had killed Hialeah and had taken my brothers. The boys had stayed with the Kiowa Indians going on five years, before the soldiers had found them. By that time, both of them could track practically anything that moved, and spoke both the Cherokee and Kiowa languages fluently. Without knowing where to find their kin, my brothers had grown up with the soldiers. Living among and learning from both Indians and soldiers had made good, strong men out of them both, and I knew Pa would be so proud. It would take time for me to know my brothers again, and it would take time

SHORT STACK

for them to know me.

CHAPTER 21
No More Secrets

Working for several hours, we finally got the inside of the cabin put back together, and there was a nice fire blazing in the fireplace. Venison was stewing in a kettle with biscuits browning over the fire. There was a smile on every face, and that made me feel warm inside, but at the same time, my heart wept bitterly for Adahy. At times my heart would just take over, memories would cross my mind, and they were bittersweet and painful. I would only shed those tears if'n I was by myself.

My brothers had vague memories of Adahy and Hialeah. Hialeah had taught me so many skills that I desperately needed, like tanning hides, cooking and—Lord, she had the staying power of a saint—when it came to teaching me sewing. We had spoken a mixed language filled with hand signals and words that only we could understand.

If'n one was upset with the other, we spoke our mind like the other one could understand perfectly. The meaning always came through, and we somehow managed to understand each other. I wanted to share so much of her with Adahy, so that he knew his Ma had been a fine woman, and she had died protecting him. My brothers and Walker used pick axes and shovels to break up the ground so Adahy could rest beside Hialeah. Walker and my brothers knew I wouldn't have had it any other way—it didn't matter none if the ground was frozen, Adahy my son would be buried proper.

I looked up over the fireplace, and Pa's fiddle was still there. I needed to wipe off the dust again, and it seemed a downright shame nobody knew how to play it.

Walker was restless. He grabbed his rifle and headed toward the cabin door. He called out over his shoulder, "I'm going to feed the horses and have a look around."

After a few moments, I followed Walker. I found him brushing down his horse, mumbling something to the animal about a mule as he stroked the brush down through its tangled mane.

"Does your horse ever answer you?"

"I don't reckon so."

I didn't know what else to say so I just stood

SHORT STACK

there, speechless for a change.

Walker finally turned to face me. He had a look like he was fixin' to speak his mind. "Short Stack, I have made my feelings known to you. I was just wondering how you'd feel about having a man around the cabin?"

My mind and heart raced, until finally what he was saying struck home. "Walker, I am *not* going to wear a dress!"

Joe's laughter filled the shed. "Not even on your wedding day? I don't reckon that's too much to ask, if'n you want to be my wife."

Before I could utter a word, he took me into his arms and kissed me like the sun wasn't coming up tomorrow. As much as I hated to admit it, Walker always took my breath away.

He placed gentle kisses all along my neck as he huskily whispered, "It'd just be for one day, Short Stack. Will you wear a dress for me on our wedding day?"

Like a lightning bolt from the blue, I found I didn't have to ponder or think on it a spell. I whispered. "Joe, I reckon I would."

Tears were threatening to spill down my face as I looked into his eyes. "You have feelings for me, but what are they, *really*?" I was feeling a mite awkward, sort of like a duck trying to talk to a bullfrog, trying to come out with just the right words, so finally I just blurted out, "Oh hell, Walker. Do you love me?"

His laughter filled my ears, and when he flashed that dumb grin across his face, I wanted to slap him. I pushed him away and turned my back to him.

Walker quickly walked up behind me, placing his large hands on my shoulders, and then gently turned me around to face him. "Short Stack, I know you're a handful, no doubt. I have always had feelings for you. Sometimes, I wanted to kiss you until the cows came home. There's times, I wanted to put you across my knee when you were stubborn as all get out. But after all's said and done, when the sun comes up tomorrow, I want to take care of you then and every day after that. I know we're going to butt heads from time to time, but you can trust me to love and protect you."

The tears that once only threatened now flowed freely down my face, but I smiled. "If you ever decide to take me across your knee you best hide my rifle first!" We walked back to the cabin together with a dumb grin on both of our faces to make known our wedding plans.

There was a cabin full of folks to look out for, but Walker and my brothers took fine care of all of us. They chopped wood, they went hunting every day, and for the first time in years, I felt

SHORT STACK

safe, as though a huge burden had been lifted off my shoulders. On days when it wasn't snowing, Walker and my brothers set about building a corral and stable for the horses. The stable was much like the cabin, except it had a door on one side where the horses could come in from the cold or wander out to the corral and stretch their legs. They even built stalls for each animal, if'n we didn't want them to go out and needed them to stay put.

I spent most of my time with Caroline, making the children moccasins out of rabbit or squirrel hides, and from the deer hides, we sewed coats. I was plumb happy with her company, and I enjoyed the sound of her laughter whenever we cooked up a meal. She taught me that the real knack of cooking was a whole lot easier than I had thought—really, just a little of this and a little of that. If I didn't have this or that then I would figure out something else to use, whatever I had at hand.

The children were a handful at times, but for the most part it was fun playing games with them, reading to them or settling their small squabbles. I never had the freedom of caring for children the way I really wanted to. I had to do what needed to be done, end of story. After David had left the mountain, everything happened fast and furious. I didn't have time to feel—I just used common sense and Pa's wisdom. I had been too stubborn to ask for help from anyone, but now I was right thankful to have the menfolk underfoot.

Joe worked right alongside of my brothers with a strong and determined mind toward protecting all of us, and every chance they got, depending on the cold, they were making it happen. If the snow and bitter cold made the menfolk stay put by the fire, they'd chew the fat on what they could do come spring—like carving small openings in the cabin walls for more rifle ports. There was also talk of digging a root cellar underneath a small portion of the cabin to store vegetables and supplies.

Cabin fever was getting the best of me, and I wanted to be embraced by the sun's light and feel the warm breath of the spring wind blowing against my face, smell the sweet blossoms of flowers and feel the warm fertile Tennessee earth beneath my feet.

The month of March has always been fickle. The warmth of the sun would bring on the first hopes of an early spring with the trees beginning to show tiny green buds. The fruit trees might even blossom—but then the weather would suddenly turn to snow and ice, shattering any hopes for an early spring.

SHORT STACK

John was healing up well and moving around some, but he was still a mite sore. Walker, Clayton and Catlin were each one about as nervous as a long-tailed cat in a room full of rocking chairs. The small cabin was closing in with four children and six grown folks, so the first day the weather was fair enough, the menfolk made a journey to the wagon the Mills family had been forced to abandon to see if'n it was still in one piece.

They took the sleds along to bring back whatever had survived the bitter cold winter. It did them a passel of good to be on a mission, and they did save the day. One of the wagon wheels had a few cracks in the wooden rim, but it survived the journey back to the cabin. Transferring some of the contents of the wagon onto the sleds, the horses were able to pull the wagon more easily. When they returned at dusk, they were a good kind of tired and hungry. They ate their fill of venison stew, golden brown biscuits and fresh apple pies Jenny had baked from the dried fruit I had stored.

Walker turned out to be quite the storyteller, spinning a good yarn for the young'uns. They hung on his every word with wide-eyes as he told them of their adventure. The menfolk were already chewing the fat over their next adventure, a trip to the trading post. First, John and Jenny needed to take the time to go through their belongings and make a list of the supplies they would need to continue on their journey, and I had to take stock of our own supplies.

I helped Jenny with the contents of their wagon, washing clothes and putting their belongings back together again. Caroline came across a bolt of soft lavender material in one of her trunks and gave it to me. I felt as if I were a butterfly softly flying across the meadow above the wild flowers as I held the cloth in my hand. Even though it would a little over a month before the birth of the first butterfly, it didn't matter, there was no doubt in my mind or in my heart this would be my wedding dress. The color of the material was that same as the wildflowers that would, before the next full moon, cover the mountain meadows, and I would be the butterfly.

Walker wanted to talk with his brother Michael about the children living at the cabin. By then, Michael Walker, a career military officer, had been promoted to colonel and was the commanding officer of the local U. S. Army outpost. We needed to leave word with the outpost just in case the children's kin came looking for them. We could tell 'em where we stumbled onto the children and give them their

SHORT STACK

first names: Suzy, Katy and Benjamin. We could tell them Suzy and Katy were sisters, but Benjamin had no other kin that we knew of.

Walker was also going to visit the preacher to see when he could make the trip up the mountain. I wanted my wedding day to be on the mountain with my family, and I wanted Molly there with me, too. Most folks at the trading post thought very little of me, but none of them really knew me. But Molly did. It was much easier to create a colorful yarn for gossip, believing the worst rather than searching for the truth of the matter.

Clayton and Catlin also needed to check in at the fort. They had given their word they'd return after they had taken care of their family, once the snow melted enough to travel down the mountain. They were trackers, and when their skills were needed, my brothers were paid well by the soldiers.

The men were excited about their journey, and once they traveled down the mountain, I knew they would be gone for several days, so Jenny helped me with my wedding dress and the children. We laughed and told each other our secrets as we cooked, read stories to the children, and sewed. The days passed by and the weather steadily settled into being blessed by the sun.

My wedding dress was almost done by the

time I finally heard the sound of the horses coming and felt the ground tremble beneath my feet. When I saw the men coming from down yonder up toward the cabin, I choked back tears of happiness. I had to be losing my mind. Why was I close to tears from being in high spirits?

The pack horses were loaded with supplies and the children ran to greet them with a smile on every little face. Walker had promised to bring them back some hard candy, and them young'uns wasn't about to leave him alone until they found the candy. The other supplies didn't matter to the young'uns. The candy came first.

The children were so happy, squealing with giggles and laughter. Joe wrapped his hands around my waist and pulled me into his arms. "Did you miss me?"

I felt the warmth of color on my face, and I rested my head a little closer to his chest. Walker roared with laughter. "Now I know how to keep you quiet." His hand softly lifted my face and his lips softly brushed mine. I was feeling so many things at once, not knowing what to do, so I let Joe take the lead, and I would follow.

Jenny and I cooked up some rabbit stew and biscuits for supper. The children jumped all over Clayton and Catlin like birds on a June bug. Walker did hear tell of folks asking about Katy

SHORT STACK

and Suzy from the trading post, and Colonel Walker had dispatched a soldier to get word to them. There had not been nary a word left about Benjamin—maybe there would never be.

There was more Walker wanted to tell me, but he wanted to talk with me alone. This had me a mite unsettled—I didn't know if it was about the wedding, my brothers or the children, but when Walker let it be known he was going to check on the horses and feed the livestock, I went with him. We walked in silence, but he took my hand in his and held on tight. When we reached the corral and walked inside, he let go of my hand and paced some across the floor before he began to speak.

"Short Stack, I heard some talk about your 'Pa' and it wasn't good. His wife up and left him, as she didn't much cotton to the mountain. Neither did her kin, so they all up and left, but your 'Pa' didn't get the same invite. David has taken it a mite hard, drinkin' and gamblin' at the saloon, and he is not good at either one. I heard tell your 'Pa' lost his shirt a time or two at the card table. Take my word for it Short Stack, these gambling men at the saloon, they are dangerous. David should know better."

I didn't want to look at Walker. I had never been much good at lying, and I had to let him know it was all right that he knew the truth about

David.

"Walker, you've known a right smart while he ain't my Pa."

"I reckon I have." Joe sighed heavily and ran his fingers through his hair as he turned to face me. "Your brothers remember David as their Pa. I didn't figure it was my place to say otherwise, so I let it be."

The thought had not crossed my mind that Clayton and Catlin would mistake David for their 'Pa.' The boys had been no bigger than corn nubbins when they had been taken from me. My brothers deserved to know the truth. I had to tell them our Pa was a good man. He didn't gamble, and while Pa took a snort every now and again, he sure as hell wasn't the man David turned out to be. It broke my heart that David had brought shame down on my Pa's good name. I could not change the past, and I wouldn't switch horses in mid-stream, but I could tell Walker the whole story, and my brothers would be told the same. Then there would be no more secrets about our Pa.

CHAPTER 22
Cherokee Roses

With Walker at my side, I had a heart-to-heart talk with my brothers. I faced Clayton and Catlin and told them the story of David's journey back to the mountain. I looked at them with a brood of butterflies spreading their wings inside my belly, my own fear doing little to calm their fluttery presence.

What would my brothers think of me once they knew the truth? I had no regrets for what I had done, until now. Joe stood solidly beside me. I was no longer alone, and I knew I could trust Walker just as I had done with Pa's love and wisdom. I was struggling to find my voice as I faced my brothers. Joe took my hand with a gentle squeeze, imparting the strength I so desperately needed. I looked my brothers straight in the eye as I fought back the butterflies that refused to be still.

Sharon A. Cantor

"Y'all was tiny enough to fit into a possum's pouch when Pa's brother David made his way up the mountain in the dead of winter. If'n it had not of been for his dog finding her way to our cabin, David would have died that day. I followed Cleo, and she led me straight to him and even helped me drag David back to the cabin. I didn't trust him right off, even though I knew he was Pa's brother. Only a damn fool or a desperate man would have traveled up the mountain in the dead of winter. Every time I tried talking to David, he wouldn't look me straight in the eye, and he avoided talking about his past. It took a spell for us to square off, circle the boundaries and trust each other, but finally he 'fessed up and told me the truth. He was kin, so I did what I thought Pa would have done. David had been young, foolhardy, and sowing wild oats—drinking, gambling, and messing with the wrong sort of folks. One night David was forced to kill a man over a woman. David caught her with another man. The man drew down on David, but he managed to clear leather first. Even after all these years, David is a wanted man. Wanted for murder.

"By the time spring arrived and the ice and snow had melted, the soldiers were able to make the journey up the mountain, and they showed up looking for David. I lied to protect him. He had done me no wrong. David taught you book learning, played with you and he loved you. I believed at the time that David had learned his lesson and if given a second chance, he would do right by Pa's name. I was wrong. Pa would be ashamed. Boys, David is not your Pa."

Clayton looked me straight in the eye with understanding and courage. He was a strong young man, but with a warm smile of mischief on his face. He came right out with it.

"Shorty, you hold the spirit of the eagle within your heart."

Catlin soothingly touched my shoulder, and when I turned to face him, he spoke right up too.

"Shorty, you have the courage of the panther."

Tears quickly filled my eyes, and damn it to hell, I couldn't stop their hot flood streaming down my face. Catlin was the closest to me, and I turned quickly and began beating both of my clenched fists over and over again into his muscular chest as I shouted at my brothers.

"Don't call me Shorty! Don't you *dare* call me Shorty! I can still bust you're backsides!"

I was slowly fading to my knees when Walker reached down and pulled me up into his arms, before my knees ever had the chance to hit the ground. As he held me close, I could hardly breathe, and I held on like the sun wasn't coming up tomorrow.

With my head buried against Walker's chest, pictures of the past flashed through my mind, one right after the other. I could see it all in my mind's eye, Pa hunting with me in the woods, Ma reading her Bible or sewing in her rocking chair, my brothers covered in molasses and feathers, Hialeah giving birth to Adahy and then the death of each one I loved. I had always believed I was strong enough to handle most anything and stand up to anyone, even those who was sure I couldn't. There was no other way for me to survive, and I could never let my guard down or ever truly feel safe enough. Joe let me throw a fit as long as I needed to, and it felt damn good. I could finally feel safe as the secrets from my past lifted from my shoulders and floated away on the delicate wings of butterflies.

My brothers reached for me at the same time, their strong arms encircling my body from both sides. Joe stepped away from me while my brothers comforted me, not saying a word—he just stood close by. I was no longer living on a prayer or dangling by the fine thread that was my stubborn pride refusing to break. I had never before let Walker see any sign of weakness. I didn't really know how I felt about that, but I was pretty sure I could get used to it.

SHORT STACK

Each day brought a new smile to my face. I was in love and I could feel the warmth of the wind on my face. With each day's passing, the mountain was coming to life with spring flowers painted across the meadows in soft colors of lavender, yellow, red and pink. The birds were chirping and singing to find a mate for their spring hatchlings. Why this thought came to mind confused me a little, as I had listened to the animals on the mountain as far back as I could remember, but I had never once thought of baby birds in the spring. I had never once stopped and listened to the squirrels chatter in the trees as the birds built their nests for their young.

I was as nervous as a bug on a hot rock, waiting for my wedding day with the coming of the next full moon. My dress was beautiful, and it made me feel downright pretty when I wore it. The dress would never have come to life without Jenny sewing it for me. Jenny was so graceful with each stitch she sewed, and I knew that was her passion.

Both of my brothers would be standing beside Joe, and I was right proud to have them with me on my wedding day. Walker had never stopped looking for my brothers, and he had kept his promise. I would love Joe Walker until the day I died, for better or worse—better on good days of laughter, and the worse being ruffled feathers when we locked horns, but there was no way around it. When I set my mind, I could be a mite stubborn, but Walker always seemed to know just what to do, whether it was a dumb grin on his face or the way he set his jaw when it was serious, and it was always in my best interests to hear him out and do it his way.

Molly would be standing beside me. I knew Molly was a real friend, she was traveling up the mountain for my wedding with a preacher sitting right next to her. He would be trying to save her soul all the way up the mountain. Molly and I sort of felt the same way about religion. Deep down, both of us figured God was there, but at times neither one of us much cottoned to what he thought seemed fair. Both of us knew too well that most pious folk couldn't see past their own noses, let alone show kindness to someone with a reputation.

Walker and my brothers were hunting for a big buck, rabbits or squirrels enough to feed everyone, while Jenny and I would be baking pies and biscuits. The wild blackberries were coming on, so we baked pies from the berries we picked or made jam. The rest we dried if we couldn't use them up fast enough, so that none went to waste.

The full moon was on my side when it graced

SHORT STACK

the sky. I could hear the wagon wheels as they creaked and whispered their hushed grumbling against the gravel and dirt as they traveled up the mountain trail for my wedding day. The menfolk all made camp just a stone's throw southeast of the cabin and passed the shine around. The next morning, even the preacher looked a little worn around the edges.

Molly and I stayed up half the night after the children had settled down and gone to sleep. We chewed the fat about men and my wedding night with giggles and secrets. It made me feel a mite better, as I was starting to feel right giddy about my wedding night. The gossip around town didn't hold no water for me, but I had never been with a man, so Molly told me the way of things.

Molly and I shared the same love for wild mountain flowers. She brought me beautiful white flowers with seven pedals and a gold center. I had not ever come across this wildflower before, and Molly told me the flowers grew wild along the Trail of Tears the Cherokee had been forced to march to the reservation.

The beautiful white blossoms of flowers was called the Cherokee Rose. The story handed down was that during the forced march, the tribal chiefs gathered together to pray for a sign to help the grieving mothers whose children were starving at their feet and suffering until their death. Something—anything—that might give the women the strength to care for their dying little ones. The Cherokee women cried with grief and prayed for their children with no moccasins on their feet in the bitter cold, no warm clothing or food.

The pure white petals of the flower signified the mother's tears as they fell to the earth. The seven petals of the white rose represented the seven families of the Cherokee tribe. The gold in the center of the white rose was the gold stolen from the mountain and the Cherokee. I felt downright honored to have those white roses mixed with the purple wildflowers of the mountain on my wedding day.

There wasn't a cloud to be seen when the sun rose in the Tennessee sky that day. I should have felt worn out, but I was so wound up my body didn't seem to know how tired it truly was. Jenny, Molly and I rustled up breakfast for everyone, a fine repast that included pancakes, venison and golden brown biscuits with honey. Clayton and Catlin had come across a bee hive in a hollow tree and they melted down the honey combs. I knew without a doubt, they'd gotten stung a few times smoking out them bees, but they never let on. The bees weren't none too happy, but on the mountain

SHORT STACK

you have to survive, and the bees would go on to make another hive.

Right after the dishes were washed, dried, put away—and the coffee ran out—the men made their way down to the meadow. The men dug a fire pit in a small meadow not far from the cabin and placed rocks and stones along the bottom. A blazing fire had been brought to life with wood piled high.

The meadow was full of purple and yellow wildflowers and their delicate scents filled the air with a delicate fragrance. The oak and elm trees surrounded the meadow on three sides, protecting the mountain flowers from the wind. It was so breathtaking and truly a scene of natural beauty. The venison had been rubbed down with honey and spices. It would be ready to cook over the open fire when the flames died down a little. The pies, the biscuits and vegetables were ready.

The girls seemed to be just as excited as I was amidst the flurry of bathing, dressing and brushing their hair. Suzy and Katy giggled and danced in a circle, wearing their new dresses with Jenny begging them to not play outside until the wedding was over. Elliott and Benjamin had gone down with the menfolk to the river for a bath before putting on their best clothes.

I put on my wedding dress, and I never felt so

beautiful. Molly and Jenny helped me with my hair, carefully arranging the purple wildflowers and the white roses in curled locks. Jenny tied a purple ribbon around the stems of the flowers to hold my wedding spray together. I couldn't wait for Joe to see me dressed up so fine, but I hoped he took a good, long gander, for I wouldn't be putting on a dress again anytime soon.

The men had returned from the river and each one was shined up like a brand new half-dime after a bath in the river and a shave. Clayton and Catlin were so handsome, even without being all shined up, and they stood tall and strong. Joe knocked on the cabin door and I opened it. He let out a loud whistle when he saw me, and reached for me, but Jenny quickly came running to push Walker out of the cabin and slam the door in his face as she scolded me.

"It's bad luck to see your intended before the wedding, child. I will fetch you when the time comes."

The time did come, and my wait was finally over. My brothers opened the cabin door, both taking my arm on either side, and they walked with me through the meadow where everyone was waiting. With Clayton on my right and Catlin on my left, I felt loved and blessed as I walked, and I knew this would forever be the happiest moment

SHORT STACK

of my life.

My brothers each kissed my cheek as they both reached for my right hand. Together they guided my hand into Joe's hand. We turned at the same time to face the preacher as my brothers walked to stand on Joe's right. At that moment, the whole world could have caught fire, and the only thing that I would have seen or felt was Joe Walker. The preacher's words echoed in my mind, and my heart beat a little faster every time Joe gazed into my eyes. Tonight, I would be lost in his arms, tonight I would be lost in his love, and I would feel the passion burn inside of me.

"Kelly Ann McDaniels, do you take Joseph Walker to be your lawful wedded husband to love, honor and cherish until death do you part?"

I was knocked back a few steps, and the preacher's words began to fade. For some reason, I was slipping to my knees, and it was getting harder and harder to breathe. How could I be falling asleep in the middle of my own wedding? I hadn't felt the bullet, nor did I hear the sound of the rifle as it fired, but I could see the blood blossoming across the front of my dress. And then I saw David.

He was standing alongside five mighty ugly, ruthless men. The children were screaming and crying, and everyone was scrambling for cover except for Joe. He was holding onto me, and I swear there was tears in his eyes.

The menfolk did not have their guns close by, as it wasn't proper during a wedding. They were making fast tracks for the children to protect them, taking cover where they could find it from the volleys of gunfire.

Pa once told me that greed couldn't abide in the heart of a good man, less'n it was invited. Once there though, greed might take a notion to make itself right at home, sleeping for a time before waking up with a vengeance when a body least expected it to. The shock of David's treachery was deep and hurtful. But I reckon greed can cause the betrayal of almost anything, even heart, home and family.

Hearing rumors of gold on Cherokee land, David had done some poking around and found gold on my mountain in the crystal-clear streams. In order to pay off his gambling debts and save his own life, David hatched himself a desperate scheme to take the mountain away from me, even if'n he had to kill me and anyone else in his way. He was a damn fool with nothing else to lose. Either way, that day his greed sealed his own fate.

Others surely would have died or at the very least would have been severely wounded if Colonel Michael Walker had not been coming up

SHORT STACK

the trail with a scouting party of soldiers, bringing kin to fetch Suzy and Katy.

Colonel Walker and his men had made short work of three of David's men, shooting them down where they stood. They captured David and one other, handing them over to Clayton and Catlin.

The preacher knelt beside me. I remember clutching his arm and whispering, "I do. Now finish it."

The preacher swallowed hard, looked into Joe's pleading eyes then softly said, "I now pronounce you man and wife. You may kiss your bride."

Walker softly kissed me and he whispered, "I love you, Short Stack."

Joe gathered me up in his arms, carried me back inside the cabin and gently laid me on the bed. He pulled the quilt up close around me, kissed me on the forehead and sat down beside me. A lifetime passed between us in those fleeting moments of a longing gaze and a loving smile. His love warmed the chill of my bones, before my sigh of contentment became a long final breath.

Walker stayed with me until my hands grew cold, and my eyes gently closed. He sat silently beside me, head bowed, his strong body shaking. It was nearly dusk when Walker strode purposefully back outside the cabin and beat David Jo McDaniels within an inch of his life.

"Miss McDaniels?" Colonel Walker asked as his brother walked away in silence, head down, fists bloodied.

Catlin looked at him defiantly. "Point of fact, Colonel, she's *Missus Walker* official now." Then he shook his head sadly, staring at the ground. "My sister's spirit has taken flight."

Colonel Walker stood silent a moment, his jaws tight. "I expect you gentlemen will see to it that justice is properly rendered." His expression saddened, and he added quietly, "You tell my brother ... if he needs anything—*anything*—he knows where to find me."

With a grim salute from the brim of his hat, Colonel Walker rode away with his men. With them went Suzy, Katy and their kinfolk, along with young Benjamin, who the folks had been willing and happy to take in.

Choking back tears of sorrow and rage, Clayton and Catlin made a noose and slung the rope it was fashioned from over a strong oak tree limb. They let David's body hang there for the vultures and varmints to chew on. He was given neither proper burial nor grave. One of the other men met the same exact fate because the soldiers' bullets had not brought him down.

SHORT STACK

The mountain would now pass legally to my brothers, who would naturally insist on sharing the care and nurturing of the land with my husband, Joe Walker. The mountain would be left in good hands.

I did know the touch of my husband. I did not ever make love to the man I loved or hold his child in my arms. Ma always allowed that the Good Book says there's a season to everything and a time to every purpose under heaven. I reckon there's the truth of ages in that. After a long winter's sleep comes springtime on the mountain, when sunlight and warm breezes whisper through the dense cover of leaves and branches like one of God's best and oldest secrets. Ever onward it goes, the seasons and years keep turnin', like the pages of a storybook that lasts forever.

To this very day, some folks say I wander the mountain in my wedding dress looking for Joe Walker. I don't reckon I'd call it wandering—I know exactly where I am. Some folks say you can hear my cries of sorrow late at night under a full moon, but I can tell you straight up—I don't cry, not anymore. I damn sure wouldn't want to scare a body—not unless they were doing wrong on my mountain.

Sharon A. Cantor

Now, if'n you're lost on the mountain and a beautiful young girl dressed in buckskin helps you find your way, or if'n an over-protective mama bear charges at you protecting her cubs. As you face the bear with your heart beating out of control and you believe this is surely your last day on earth. But suddenly, the bear stops dead in her tracks, roars at a sudden gust of wind and then runs in the opposite direction, well, it just might be your lucky day.

Or it just might be a mountain woman known as Short Stack.

ABOUT THE AUTHOR

Sharon Cantor was born in Sinton, Texas. One of five siblings, she grew up in Lebanon, Indiana. She is a graduate of Northwood University located in South Florida, where she now resides. Her many interests include her love of the ocean, shell collecting, country music, antique dolls, NASCAR racing and football.

Sharon is also the author of **Two Hearts, One Song** available at Amazon.com

Made in the USA
Charleston, SC
20 February 2016